Story of a Marriage

2

I NEED TO REMEMBER HOW THINGS WERE FOR her that spring. In the days before it all happened. She was a woman in the prime of life. She could walk confidently into any room or situation. For her a crowd was like a friendly forest, she mingled easily, able to talk to anyone and everyone. She'd always had long hair, but after getting together with me she cut it short and dyed it black. At night she'd sleep on her side, one hand tucked under her cheek. I lay behind her, my arms around her, both of us naked, and she'd feel the warmth of my front against her back. At night-time it was just the two of us; in the morning we'd wake on our own side of the bed. She was usually woken by the children, or by me. The rooms were light, our voices soft. There's a long period that can only be remembered as a time of happiness, both unlooked for and undeserved. We used to sit together around an oval dining table, Danish design, made of steel and white Respatex. The table was far too expensive for us that Saturday when we bought it, but we got used to that, the debts mounted and we barely gave it

1

– TELL ME ABOUT *US*.

  – About us?

  – Tell me as though I knew nothing.

  – Well, we were lovers.

  – Yes. And then?

  – We got married. We were husband and wife.

  – And then?

  – We were a mum and dad. We had children together.

  – Not that. Tell me about *us*. What happened between *us*?

  – We lived together.

  – And did we take care of each other?

  – What do you mean? Yes, we did.

  – But then one day.

  – Then one day? You want me to tell you about that?

  – I need to hear what happened between us. I don't understand it.

  – I'm not too clear about it all myself.

  – Can't you try to tell me about it anyway?

  – I don't think I can. No, I don't want to. I can't.

  – Do you want me to tell it instead? Then I will.

1 3 5 7 9 10 8 6 4 2

Hogarth, an imprint of Vintage,
20 Vauxhall Bridge Road,
London SW1V 2SA

Hogarth is part of the Penguin Random House group of companies whose
addresses can be found at global.penguinrandomhouse.com.

Penguin
Random House
UK

First published by Hogarth in 2018
Published by agreement with Copenhagen Literary Agency ApS, Copenhagen
First published in Norway by Aschehoug, as *Historie om et ekteskap*, in 2015

This translation has been published with the financial support of NORLA

NORLA
NORWEGIAN LITERATURE ABROAD

penguin.co.uk/vintage

A CIP catalogue record for this book is available from the British Library

ISBN 9781784741600

Typeset in India by Integra Software Services Pvt. Ltd, Pondicherry
Printed and bound by Clays Ltd, St Ives Plc

Penguin Random House is committed to a sustainable future for our
business, our readers and our planet. This book is made from
Forest Stewardship Council® certified paper.

Story of a Marriage

GEIR GULLIKSEN

Translated from the Norwegian
by Deborah Dawkin

HOGARTH
LONDON · NEW YORK

a thought. We sat at that table, morning and evening, the kids did their homework there. Later the table would be too big; it went to her and the kitchen in which she put it was smaller. She sold it in the end, and now it stands in somebody else's house; the table has a new life, like everything else we once shared.

She cycled beneath light leafy canopies. She breathed with an open mouth. She ran up the stairs, whenever she had to go up a floor, which was often. She never took the lift, she hated to stand still. This particular morning she was giving a presentation for staff in another department. It went well, she could feel she had them with her (their faces turning towards her like fresh green shoots waking to the light). Afterwards the communications director was keen to make another booking with her. They agreed to exchange emails, and several people came up and thanked her for the talk. And then, on her way out, she spotted a man who made her stop. She didn't know why. She just stopped and watched him as he made his way through the crowd, his gaze fixed on her. His eyes, there was something about them, something mild but insistent, confident but searching, she wasn't sure what. Even later, when it was all over, she didn't know what it had been, she couldn't explain it, not even to herself, and certainly not to me.

He was tall and stood out, though not just because of his height. He had a long face with slightly slanted eyes, his skin was marked with tiny scars, acne as a teenager perhaps. Not exactly handsome, it has to be said, although I can scarcely be objective. Yet there was something seductive and intriguing about those eyes, or his smile perhaps, or the tilt of his head. She waited for him to reach her, and he smiled as he approached, pushing his way determinedly through the others who were filing out of the room. She felt rather hot, she didn't know why. Moments later they stood looking at each other, and she hoped that her face expressed a mildly amused curiosity: what had he come to say? Her face should convey that she had been held up and had no idea what he might want, but that she was prepared to give whatever it was her considered attention. He started talking. Something about public health, her own specific area of interest. He said things she might have said herself, although she thought he phrased them better. Or did he? His way of speaking was vaguely awkward, as though he was attempting to follow her perspective, but was incapable of letting go of his own. This last comment is, of course, a vast over-interpretation on my part – I don't need to be told, I can see it myself. No, she probably found his comments both enriching and stimulating. He walked out of the room with her, accompanied her all the way down the stairs. They walked to her bicycle, still talking as she unlocked it and got ready to go.

Afterwards she cycled slowly through the streets, she had to get back to the office, but she took her time. The world seemed to want to show off for her that morning: the maple trees or lime trees (she didn't much care what kind they were) seemed to spread their branches for her, a glossy magpie elegantly flicked its tail, young leaves stirred in an otherwise imperceptible breeze. She was happy. Contented in herself and her life. Every living thing opened itself up for her wherever she went.

She was afraid of nothing.

Once she had been a young girl, now she was a middle-aged woman. She was twenty-five when she first met me, it was a long time ago now, and I was just a few years older.

I called her Timmy. She had another name, an ordinary girl's name, that she didn't really like. And then one evening, a month or so into our relationship, we were lying in bed in her old apartment watching *Timmy Gresshopper* on TV. We weren't actually watching anything, we'd been in bed for hours on end, we had got up to eat and then gone back to bed, we'd been obsessing over each other for so long, investigating what our bodies could do together, and we needed a break. We drank water, and I flicked through the channels, past an old Disney cartoon – she asked me to stop and go back. We watched it and we both found it touching, though it was me who cried. I had a young child whom I wouldn't see that day, that entire week, because I chose to be here in bed with her. That was why I cried, she knew that. But she pretended to believe I was moved by the film, and told me afterwards that she'd always liked *Timmy Gresshopper*, better than *Snipp og Snapp*, better even than Dumbo or Pinocchio. She identified with Timmy, because he always tried to make the best out of everything, he'd take his umbrella and go for a walk, singing as he went, eternally earnest and optimistic, even when darkness closed around him and he had no idea where he was.

5

– That's you, I said. – You *are* Timmy. Always wanting to put things right, and never giving up on your goals.

I was full of admiration for her already then. It was my way of loving her. She didn't understand that until later, and for a long time she felt overwhelmed by how amazing she was in my eyes. She replied that she'd never thought of herself as a grasshopper, and I came up with some flirtatious joke about liking the way she rubbed her hind legs against mine. Meaningless, it wasn't even funny, and she could see I instantly regretted it, that I felt embarrassed, and that I wasn't in the habit of talking that way. She'd loosened me up, she realised, and that moved her, or inspired feelings of love, if there's a difference between the two. After that night I started calling her Timmy. It stuck, it went beyond being a nickname, it became her name, the name everyone used, our friends and even her work colleagues.

Back in her office she was sitting in the light from her screen. She was going through a report. She'd been working on it for ages, but today it was going better. She was very focused, giving it her complete attention, not opening any emails or checking the news. She gazed out of the window onto the kindergarten below, at the children playing in the sandpit, but her thoughts were on the report. She was unsure about one or two of the tables, the figures didn't add up. She kicked her shoes off under the desk, rubbed her bare feet against each other. She stroked her hand over her neck, a caress almost. Her other hand drifted under her blouse and touched her belly, she let her hand wander up to her bra and fiddled with one of the straps.

The telephone rang. She had to free her hand to take it. It was a colleague who was at home with a sick child, calling to ask her to send him a document. She searched for it on the intranet and emailed it to him. Then picked up from where she'd been interrupted. Her thoughts drifted to supper, and me. She thought about public health policy, then cycling, and whether it would be dry enough in the forest to go cycling that weekend. She might go alone, or with the kids. Preferably alone. She wanted to cycle fast, to challenge herself. It occurred to her that it was only Tuesday. She looked up at the clock. She had worked solidly for an hour. She wondered if she should go for a pee, but decided to work straight through to lunch. She considered asking Kjersti to look through a few sections of the report. But then changed her mind, she'd rather manage it alone. She was ambitious and worried about being seen as insecure or weak. A shadow flickered across her screen. Outside the window a heavy crow flapped, heading for the tree near the kindergarten. It landed on a thin branch, and perched there for a while rocking. She would wait before talking to Kjersti. Try to get a bit more done first. The crow moved to a thicker branch, spread its feathers and cocked its head; it was watching the children below, small motionless figures, barely two years old, sitting in the sandpit, each clasping a spade pointed downwards at the sand, making no attempt to dig, they'd not learned that yet.

She raised her arms in the air and took a long stretch. Her blouse rode up, revealing her bare stomach. She thought about the man she'd spoken to earlier. She was certain he'd flirted with her. She hadn't flirted back, but she'd been very friendly and open, he must have noticed. She'd enjoyed talking to him. She liked his hands. She imagined them on her thighs; slightly rough manly hands against her smooth pale skin. She liked her thighs, these days at least, she hadn't before, on the contrary, they'd been too skinny, but since she'd begun running her thighs were stronger, more muscular. She could feel her inner thigh muscles now, even though she was sitting still. She decided she'd tell me later that evening about the man who had approached her after her talk. I was sure to approve. And she liked what happened between us when she told me about other men she had looked at, or men who had looked at her. She knew I liked to hear about it. She didn't understand why exactly, but that wasn't important, she didn't feel the need to analyse everything.

She got up and went out into the corridor. She'd forgotten she was barefoot and went back in and shoved her feet into her shoes. She decided to see Kjersti after all, she'd been helpful in the past. Kjersti's door was open and her office was empty, but the computer was still on. She'd go for a pee and Kjersti might get back in the meantime. It was quiet in the corridor, people were at meetings out of house. She walked past reception, smiled at the woman sitting there, a temp. She wondered if she should stop and say something, but didn't want to lose concentration. She went into the loo and locked the door, paused in front of the mirror. She felt good, although her hair was a little too long. She wanted to do something with it. Get a new cut and slightly new colour. She wondered if she should start using make-up. A touch of eyeliner

8

couldn't hurt, I wouldn't like it, but I'd get used to it eventually. She sat down, listened to her piss as it chattered noisily into the water below. What pleasure. The pleasure of peeing hard, the pleasure of wiping yourself slowly and meditatively, the pleasure of getting dressed again, of packing yourself into your clothes like a child in the morning, and then washing your hands. Washing your hands and sniffing them, the delicate scent of soap and damp skin.

She was on her way out, but changed her mind and returned to the mirror. She studied her face as she slid her hand down into her trousers. They were too tight, she unzipped them and pulled them down. She touched herself, guiding two fingers to the slippery smoothness that belonged to the inner surface of her body. It was difficult to reach with your trousers round your knees, but she liked that too, that it was tight and difficult. She moved her fingertips and watched her reflection. A faint blush rose on her cheeks. She thought about the report. She thought about whether she'd be able to come as she stood here touching herself in front of the mirror at work. Probably not. It would take something rather special at least. A few vague images of naked bodies flashed up, only to fade.

Might it have been like that? No, I'm going too far, this all just points back to me, to my repertoire, to my habitual register, not to hers at all. It was probably more like this: She went quickly to the toilet, thought only of the report, glanced briefly at herself in the mirror as she washed her hands. Thought her face looked somehow different, but wasn't sure why. Somebody passed by in the corridor outside, she stood there for a moment and waited for the footsteps to disappear. It went quiet.

It clicked for her, she suddenly knew precisely what was needed; she opened the door and walked briskly down the corridor. Kjersti's office was still empty, which was just as well; she returned to her own office and was back at work before she had even sat down. She would print out the entire report and go through it from the very beginning one more time. The basic premise was unclearly formulated, and had been from start. She went to the printer, hoping not to meet anyone on the way. The corridor was empty, the printer hummed and the friendly warm pages landed straight in her hand. She felt the urge to sing. But she rarely sang now, not since the kids had got bigger. She felt the urge to break into a run, saw herself sprinting up a long, steep staircase, and at the top of this staircase was nothingness. She ran all the way up, but didn't want to turn back, it was like an image in a movie, in a dream, in a movie that imitated a dream. The corridor was long and empty, she heard footsteps behind her, she turned to check if she was alone. She sat down in her office again with the pages in her lap. She kicked off her shoes, pushed her chair back and put her feet on the table. She had large feet, she liked that, and liked to go barefoot, liked to sit and spread her toes.

She was hungry, and lunch was an hour away, so she ate an apple. Gnawed her way to the core, then put it on the windowsill. There were already two wrinkled apple cores sitting there, she couldn't have left anything like that on the windowsill at home, and she liked to do so here. She allowed herself to be messy, freeing herself from my demands for clean and tidy tables and worktops. Suddenly she heard voices outside her office, the colleagues who had been out at meetings were returning. She listened to their footsteps, the busy rustling of bags and jackets, snippets of conversation floating down the corridor, and she recognised each voice.

She put her feet back on the floor and pulled her chair closer to the screen. She reopened the document and started to insert the corrections she'd made by hand. She resisted the desire to say hello to anyone passing, she didn't want to talk now. She sat so they would see she was working. She concentrated so hard on looking concentrated that she lost concentration altogether. She felt the urge to give up. She felt an urge to go out and get some air. She felt an urge to google the name of the man she'd talked to that morning. She got up and went down to Kjersti's office. She still wasn't there. She remembered that Kjersti had said she was going to the doctor's. Timmy went back to her own office, she had decided to take a break, and the first thing she did was check her emails. Not that she ever used the word email, she just said mail; I tried to get her to say email, but everybody at work said mail these days, so why shouldn't she? Why be complicated when there was a simple alternative? So, she checked her mail, and didn't find much, apart from an *email* from me.

I wrote that I was thinking about her, and thinking about what we'd done a few hours earlier. She'd forgotten, but now she pictured it, she'd been down on all fours, supporting herself on her elbows while I took her hard from behind, the way she liked. I'd held her hips, then

11

moments later she'd felt my hand on the nape of her neck, as I shoved her face down into the bed. She remembered her own voice now, yelling into the pillow. She liked to hear herself scream. I *took* her, she let herself be *taken*, she screamed. She liked to think of it like that, of *being taken*. We had looked at ourselves in the mirror, two bodies, one on top of the other, one doing something to the other, the other allowing itself to be done to. And as she pictured it now she felt it between her legs, a dull ache.

She sent a reply, brief, affectionate and in much the same spirit as I'd written to her. That was how we always wrote to each other. She looked out over the kindergarten, one of the little figures turned in her direction, peering up towards the sky perhaps, although it felt as though its gaze was searching for her window. I had said that I wouldn't mind more children. She didn't want more, absolutely not, we'd gone past that phase long ago. We already had two children together, as well as my daughter from my first marriage, that would have to be enough. She wanted to work more. She wanted to do more sports, to run and cycle, to learn how to climb. She wanted to take advantage of everything on offer to a mature person who no longer had young children to look after.

Her other emails included a notification of a forthcoming meeting, and some contributions to a discussion about the Department of Health website. She considered sending a response to the last, but decided instead to delete it. The joy of eradicating little problems. She sent an email to Kjersti asking, in the humorous tone they usually adopted in their communications, whether she could be *an angel and help her go through the tables in that pesky report.* She had worked on it for so long now that the report had developed a personality. An awkward individual that refused to take shape as she wanted, there was always something wrong with it. She'd talked about it so much, that I often enquired about it: *How's the report doing these days?*

We often talked about work, especially hers. She'd grown used to sharing everything with me. Almost everything: conflicts, negotiations, minor irritations, and also, of course, anything she found interesting or amusing or inspiring. Always a positive soul, she was consciously so, she wanted to be that positive person, and it came easily.

She checked the news, informing herself lightly, without any real commitment. Then another email arrived. She opened it. She didn't recognise the sender immediately, not before she'd begun reading. He thanked her, and was warm and complimentary about her talk, she could almost hear his voice, the friendly tone, the interest, the charm, or whatever it was. Yet there must have been something conditional behind this charm, behind all the praise and positive words, she sensed something else: he wasn't giving himself away. She picked up on a certain reserve, a slightly aggressive tension. And it triggered something in her. Or, perhaps he was just self-obsessed, he wrote mostly about what *he* thought, and obviously felt sure it would be of interest to her. He went on to suggest they might collaborate, that there was a project in the offing in his division which he'd like her to be involved in. She was, against her will, flattered by that too, even though she had neither the time nor desire to participate in any more projects. Finally he said, by the by, that they lived very near each other. He'd recognised her when she was up on the podium, but hadn't known where he knew her from. But this must be why, they were practically neighbours. Perhaps she was a jogger too, like himself? He was almost certain she must be, he wrote. He was quite certain he'd seen her out jogging.

So, he had googled her to find out where she lived, perhaps at the very moment she'd considered googling him. He had found her address, but that wasn't all. He must have seen her before, seen her out running. Could he see from her body that she often went running?

He'd used the word *jogger* – who used that nowadays? It was so nineties, so eighties, almost awkward. It reminded her of his glasses, their brown-tinted lenses. She did a search on his name, and was surprised to find he was older than she'd thought. He didn't live far from us, she knew exactly which house it was, she'd often run past it. She tried to remember if she'd ever seen him before. She looked at the pictures of him and recognised something in them that had made an impression on her earlier. A look of vulnerability. A self-confidence, which nonetheless seemed somehow brittle. She found more pictures, one on the department's home page, another from an interview with a professional journal. And then more on the website of a sports club.

He was a ski instructor.

She sat, staring into space and thinking she wouldn't mind doing that herself.

She got a fright when Kjersti suddenly came up behind her, she'd not heard her come in.

– What a face!

She wanted to close the page, but it would look too conspicuous, as though she had something to hide. Instead she swung her chair round and fixed Kjersti's gaze, forcing her attention away from the screen and onto herself.

– You terrify me when you come up so quietly.

– Martin always says I stomp about like a horse.

– That's nice of him.

– Well, we've got so many stairs at home, you see. And he says I breathe like a whale.

– I'm sure he loves you anyway.

– I don't really think he does. He's just holding out and waiting for something to happen. Every time I go to the doctor, he hopes it'll be something serious. He's so vain he'd rather be a widower than get a divorce. But you've got a husband who loves you, that's obvious. And yet, you're looking at that man?

– He wants me to work on a project that's being led by Health and Social Care.

– Aha, a *project*! Is that what they call it these days?

– It's totally innocent, Kjersti. Strictly professional.

– And you believe that?

– Kjersti, I need your help.

– Is that report of yours still bugging you?

– I think there are a few errors in those tables.

– Can't you just send them back to whoever created them?

– I'm responsible for the report. I'm wondering if the basic premise is faulty.

– Show me these errors then.

Kjersti pulled the visitor's chair up to the screen. They often sat side by side, working together. Timmy often talked about Kjersti to me, about her sailboat, about her marriage, about the awful jokes, the nitpicking, the way she got hung up on details. And she talked to Kjersti about me too. She must have, I'm not sure what about exactly, but I always assumed she talked about her wonderful marriage. And very likely she did. We were proud of our marriage, both of us, like parents pushing their newborns out in their prams, parading them for all the world to see, as though nobody else had ever experienced such joy.

She closed the websites she'd visited, she closed her email account and brought the report up again. For the rest of the day she sat and worked with Kjersti. She left the office a bit later than planned. She knew I'd be at home, but she texted me to say she was on her way.

And that she loved me. She must have said that – didn't we always? She can't quite remember now. The person she was then, when she was with me, no longer exists. The person I was with her no longer exists. A 'we' once existed, we lived together, but that life is now over and she has forgotten who we were. She is beyond the reach of what happened, as am I. Nobody knows any more how the two of us, she and I, once spoke with each other. Who was she, when she was with me? She remembers how my gaze would follow her. How when she walked through a room, I would sit and watch her. She would sometimes sit and watch me too, but never for so long or so often. But she remembers how our eyes would meet, without anything in particular happening, without anything being said. What did our glances say? That we were happy with our lives, with each other, that things had worked out pretty well? We'd found each other, we'd built a life together, and she liked who she was with me.

She looked upon me with familiarity and almost dreadful tenderness. Though it didn't seem dreadful to me, or even to her, not back then. It was only later that she came to see our exchange of tenderness as precisely that: a mode of exchange, something we traded with one another, in payment for one another's closeness.

There he was, this man who was her husband, in this house, in these rooms, following her with his eyes whenever she walked past. She no longer remembers my face, she can't picture it, apart from when we meet accidentally. She can't recall how my face always turned to hers, how steadfast and open that gaze was. She knows it must have been so, that she was watched over, with kindness, openness, admiration, adoration. But she has no recollection of what it was like to live under that gaze, that face.

She cycled home in the late-afternoon traffic. Usually she cycled as fast as she could, partly for the exercise, and partly because she hated to be overtaken. But also because she looked forward to getting home. But not today. She looked at her hands, there on the handlebars, at her feet on the pedals, at the blotched asphalt beneath her wheels. She was in no hurry. She arrived home, got off her bike and wheeled it through the gate, put it away and locked it up, then walked slowly across the gravel. Something, something was pulling her back. The large courier bag in her hand was stuffed with papers including a printout of the report which she planned to go through tonight, to keep the work that she and Kjersti had done fresh in her mind for the next day. She passed by the kitchen window and saw me standing at the worktop. She could hear that the children were home too, further back in the room. She could smell that the dinner was ready, there was music on the radio, all the doors and windows were open.

Something was holding her back, but she pushed it aside. She can't remember what she wore. She can't remember if she was wearing a dress, the short-sleeved dress perhaps, because summer was on its way, or the thin dress with red and green spots. Or perhaps it was the denim one that I'd bought for her. Or the one with dark blue and light blue stripes. Or the red and green dress, with a collar and a thin belt that tied at the waist. Or the plain red one that was cut too low at the neck, surely she wouldn't have worn that when she was giving a talk? She was wearing a suit, the pastel skirt that reached just above the knee, together with a blouse. One of her white blouses, or the brown one, the one that shimmered, with an embroidered collar. It was rather tight, that one, the fabric stretched between the buttons, revealing her pale skin beneath. A bit risqué, she often thought, but she sometimes wore it anyway. She may, of course, have worn trousers and a T-shirt; her linen trousers with the lilac T-shirt, the one with a floral print. She bought more expensive clothes these days, always knew exactly which shop every garment came from, and whether she'd bought it herself or been given it, although she wasn't thinking about that now. She may have been wearing her short-sleeved dress, the pale one that looked like a blouse on top, with a stiff collar, the one with pleats below, that came out quite wide round the knees, like a skirt. The advantage of this dress was that it went so well with the grey jacket she liked so much, the one Kjersti called her power-jacket.

But that's enough of that.

She came home, walked in to me and the kids, we'd been waiting for her, as we so often did. We liked it better when she was at home, seeing her made us happy, each in our own ways. I was standing at the kitchen worktop, I turned to her, she could see that I went soft at the sight of her, that I was moved, hazy with tenderness. I walked over to her and put my arms round her, she reciprocated my embrace, lightly, feeling no more than an easy, numb sense of pleasure. The attentive devotion that greeted her, many would have craved, many were obliged to live without. She had lived with that tenderness and care for so long, she was accustomed to it, some might say she was spoiled. Or perhaps she was just beginning to get bored. She was about to move on, out of our world, the one we had together, and into something else. But she didn't know that yet, nor that I could not reach her. *Oh, what a waste*, she would throw it away, everything.

We were here, in these rooms. Our voices could be heard, our bodies sat on chairs, lay on beds, our hands reached out and adjusted the thermostat, picked up telephones, carried cups and saucers. She dozed on the sofa,

19

then woke again. I sat reading. One of us helped the youngest boy with his homework. She watched TV, I read more or wrote, she leafed through her paperwork, we sat side by side on the sofa talking in clear, sincere voices. She told me what had happened at work, an argument in management. Then she told me about the man she'd met. I asked, she answered, it was light and fun, I laughed at her description of him, the stiff shirt, with the wide, loudly patterned tie, she talked about it all so amusingly, without putting him down. She knew, as she talked, that she was portraying him in a charming light, and that it was kind of exciting – it was exciting that she'd never known anything about this man, and that he was suddenly there, so close to us, with his wide tie and white shirt, and that he wanted something to do with her.

A little later she went into another room and talked on the phone, it was her sister. She was interrupted by our youngest, she called out to me, called my name, the way she always did. And she said to him *ask Daddy* and resumed her conversation. Something had happened, her sister was in the middle of getting divorced. We had both been rather upset by it, and we might have felt threatened, but didn't. We weren't there yet, we thought we were safe in our life together. The kitchen had been tidied, the lights had been gradually lit as darkness fell. They would soon be turned off again, one by one.

We headed for bed, stood side by side in the bathroom brushing our teeth, she put her hand on my shoulder, companionably, smiled at me in the mirror. We lay in bed naked. She turned towards me, I turned towards her.

A hand on a thigh, a cheek on a shoulder, a hand at the nape of a neck, fingers through hair. One mouth opened towards the other mouth, one body lay on the other. One of us let out a scream, soon the other joined it. Our voices in that little room triumphed over loneliness, or so it seemed. And yet, when she remembered those voices later, yelling at the ceiling in the dark, they seemed plaintive, searching and alone. As though we each shouted out our own distress.

The next day she shoves her feet into her trainers, ties her laces, calls out to tell me or the kids that she'll be away for an hour. And she closes the door behind her. It can't have been the next day, some days must have passed, but those days have been erased from her mind. Like most of our life together: totally erased. She no longer remembers it. All she remembers is that first meeting with him, and then the second, and the third. And then she remembers how everything fell apart around her.

It was late in the afternoon, the sun was low, she'd changed into her running gear and now she crossed the gravel path full of anticipation. She had a habit of expecting the best. And everything had gone her way. She closed the gate behind her and started to run, gently at first, along the road where we lived. Reaching the end of the road, she slipped like a child through a gap in the fence which led into the forest. She'd be able to run more freely. Initially she was met by walkers and children, and had to stop or go round them, but as she went further into the forest she could gather pace.

The forest path was soft and spongy underfoot. She could hear her own breath, her pulse throbbed in her temples, her shoulder ached. All of this would give way as soon as she was warm, she knew that, longed for it, looked forward to running without thinking about running. She took the footpath that skirted the residential area. She often went deeper into the forest, where the houses vanished from view, where the forest floor broke into an intricate web of tiny paths, but today she wanted to be out in the open, because – she told herself – the light was so beautiful here.

And so, as though in a dream in which everything went to a plan, a plan she didn't recognise as such until afterwards, she ran past the little villas with their gardens overlooking the forest. The man who had emailed her lived in one of them, and she recognised it instantly. A small 1960s house, not very well maintained, but with a neat stack of logs in the carport. An old hammock in the garden, and a snow shovel that hadn't been taken in after the winter. They hadn't lived here long, two or so years perhaps, and they'd moved straight in without doing anything to the house, he wasn't concerned with such things, she had realised.

And there, outside the house, just as she had imagined, she saw him. She hadn't known that she was hoping for this, but realised it now; this was exactly how he should stand, as though waiting for her. He'd been out for a run too, and now he was stretching. He was focused, serious and sure of himself, not looking to the left or right. But still he spotted her. They saw each other from afar, and he recognised her and lifted a hand to wave. As though he'd been waiting for her. His hand in the air, she'd remember that, and his face as she approached him. His eyes went narrow and more slanted whenever he smiled, she noticed that.

He leapt over the stone wall and waited for her on the road. Straight to it. As usual, she thought, even though she didn't know him yet. But she already knew what was typical of him, recognising it the instant she saw it, and he said:

– Going far?

She was friendly but to the point, she wanted to be sporty and down-to-earth, and it came easily to her, it felt somehow right to her, and she sensed that it felt right to him too. The two of them were already starting to build a rapport. She named a place. It would take barely an hour to run there and back, but he'd just been out for a run, so she didn't expect him to join her. She asked anyway, and he said:

– I'd love to.

With an almost gallant wave of the arm he gestured for her to lead the way. And she obeyed, if that's the right word, she wasn't one to take orders. But still. It felt as though he'd taken control, even though she'd been the one to invite him. She ran in front and could hear him coming up behind. It took time for her to find her own rhythm, it was as though she was somehow *being run* – my phrase, I'd used it once when I'd been on the treadmill in the gym. I came home and told her that I'd felt invaded upon by the exercise machines, it had felt like *being run*, rather than

23

running for myself. Typical of me, she'd thought, that I could feel invaded upon even by a treadmill. Not that she thought of that now. She ran ahead on the path, in front of a man she didn't know, and felt his gaze upon her.

She ran faster to take back control. She felt strong. He was certainly stronger than her, she knew that, she'd already noticed how fit he was. His thighs in those shorts were better than she'd imagined. Nonetheless she heard him start to breathe more heavily, and she upped her pace to give him something to work against. He must have noticed, and liked it, she thought. They were challenging one another. They ran for a long time without a word, without her even turning her head. But she knew that she had him close behind her. His trainers pounded the ground, she could hear his breath, could sense the volume of his upper body, the capacity of his lungs. He sounded well built, a little heavy. He was taller than me, she'd noticed that immediately. She ran with an easy stride, taking long leaps when she felt like it, jumping from side to side where it was rocky, but she started to tire, and that annoyed her, she didn't want to let him pass her.

She was pretty certain he was looking at her arse, she felt his gaze like a warm hand, checking it out, first one buttock, then the other. She thought she could feel his eyes scan downwards. She reached a clearing where the path got wider, and slowed down so he could run up beside her.

And instead, he ran right past her.

That was typical too. She knew that already. That was, of course, how things would be between them. Solid competition, honest rivalry, no sentimental niceties. They played, but there was always a serious challenge behind everything they did. He sped on, with no intention of making it easy for her. She was well behind him, the gap widening more than she liked. But then she gained more ground than she thought she'd manage. He must have relented a little, after all, because suddenly she was right behind him again. They were running uphill, his arse looked firm, tighter, harder than hers, just as it should be. But his thighs were strangely hairless, she could see his muscles working under his brown skin. His back was long, she observed the slender nape of his neck, the slightly strained sinews in his throat. He wore a wedding ring, somebody else was married to him and lay under him, put their hands on his back, touched him. She already disliked the idea that anybody else could do this.

But perhaps she wasn't aware of that herself. After all, nothing was out in the open yet, she was still just in a state of suspense. Their attraction worked its way in secret, feeding itself on anything and everything. He ran with his palms open, and she felt a vague tenderness towards those hands, the way he held them out in front of him.

Suddenly he stopped and, turning towards her, said there was something he wanted to show her. He left the path and pushed aside some thin branches, holding them back long enough for her to pass. She followed him up a hill. He knew this forest, he told her later, like the back of his hand, and she stored this up, used the same expression when she told me about it. What an idiotic expression, the disproportionate comparison between a vast landscape and the back of a hand, such an illogical and worn-out expression was the best she could offer me then. She followed him uphill until there were no more trees, only shrubs and bare rock, and then further still where the rocks were loose and it was increasingly difficult to walk. He used the opportunity to take her hand and help her up the last little stretch; she accepted his hand and felt it close around hers and thought to herself, she must have, that this was the first time.

He took her hand and pulled her up towards him. They sat down on the top of the hill, on a flat boulder, and squinted over the forest in the fading sun. Not over the city, nor over the fjord, nor even a little lake. All they could see was mile upon mile of forest. Dark fir trees, slightly lighter pines, and the occasional belt of dazzling green deciduous forest. The patchwork shades of a mixed woodland. Hills, plateaus, ridges and dips, covered in an infinite number of trees in a multitude of greens.

This was what he had wanted to show her.

An unbelievable sight for her, a view she had never imagined existed. They sat quite close, she was still breathing heavily from running. As was he, thankfully. She felt his skin against hers, their legs touching. He pulled his leg away. She followed him, letting her knee swing out so that her leg touched his again. This time he didn't pull back. For a long time they sat like that as he talked about the places where he used to run. He pointed out landmarks, told her stories of how he'd got lost, about trips he'd taken. It was as if he owned everything he pointed at, as if he had laid claim to it all, made it his own.

Could she tell from his voice that it did something to him to sit so close to her? She drew back her leg so it wouldn't be too obvious, so he wouldn't misunderstand. She was a happily married woman, just enjoying the pleasure of getting to know a man who had shown her some interest. She looked at his arms, his forearms, they were brown and coarse like a leather belt. Perhaps she wanted to put her hand on his arm. Perhaps she already knew what it would feel like. She felt soft and lithe, and stronger than she had for a long time. She felt a faint tremor in her body and she wondered if it came from him. Large hands. He bit his nails, not a lot, but enough for each nail to be embedded in the flesh of his fingertips. She'd never have thought she could like that, but she did. She sat thinking about how she would come home and tell me about him. She was already looking forward to seeing my face, she knew I'd be surprised.

3

SHE WAS A MATURE WOMAN WHEN SHE TOOK up running. She ran along dusty roads covered with a thin layer of sand, on tarmac darkened by rain, and on gravel paths in the little forest near the house. She ran long distances, ran until she reached the narrowest forest paths, where her steps pounded softly, vibrant, alive, almost echoing back at her from the forest floor, where thin roots spread skeletal in the dry sandy soil. She still wasn't as fast as she wanted to be; too many people overtook her. And eventually her feet would grow heavy, her trainers would strike the ground with a dead thud. She'd want to lie down and never get up again. But she went on running. She ran up flights of stairs and steep hills, she began interval training, pushing herself until she gasped with exhaustion. She watched the others that ran, modelled herself on them, modelled herself on anyone who ran effortlessly through the world.

She wanted to achieve that too. She bought lighter trainers, trainers that didn't hit the ground so heavily and with such resignation. She was already faster. She launched herself from the balls of her feet and thrust herself forward. She launched herself and started to sprint — no, not yet, she ran as though she was bursting, ran to distance herself from everything she had once been. She'd already forgotten that she'd ever been slow, sluggish and unfit. She overtook long-legged women in Lycra and super-fit men in shorts. She liked to pick out the fittest men, liked to position herself behind them and then tail them for a while before sprinting past, and finally upping her pace even more after she'd overtaken them. She made it obvious to everyone that she would never submit. And she loved it, this feeling that she could outdo anyone, well, not quite anyone, but *almost* anyone she pitted herself against. That she set the pace knowing they had to give way, had to adjust to her speed and settle behind her. That she ran at the front, and that anyone else, whoever they were, had to run behind. She'd always been the one who had to stand aside and watch others, now she was the one to be watched.

She ran to hold out, to keep the everyday despondency and despair at bay. And we undressed each other, touched each other, sucked and licked each other, in tender or violent sexual encounters to hold out, to get through the day's boredom and chaos and exhaustion. We had children together to hold out, and to make our world richer and less predictable. We went on holiday, celebrated birthdays and Christmas, lay close together at night, helped each other get up in the morning, all to make life into more than just a case of holding out. We touched each other gently or greedily, we fantasised together about things that might bring unexpected intimate pleasures, we maintained a ceaseless flirtation with each other, all in order, if possible, to beautify life. What else should we have done?

When our windows were open in the evening we'd hear the sound of other runners, their rapid and rhythmic footsteps on the gravel path or tarmac outside. Sometimes she'd drift off to sleep listening to them. There was a quiet and gentle enthusiasm in the sound of those feet pushing so swiftly and lightly against the ground, the sound of purposeful and solitary pleasure; one by one they ran in the twilight, building their strength and ability to hold out.

She ran every day. At first she ran with music in her ears, but soon stopped. Now she heard only her own breath, gasping and eager. Her face reddened, her scalp grew hot, her hands ached. Why should her hands ache? She didn't know, but they did. Her mouth gaped open as she ran. She ran for an hour at a time, she could have run all day, she was tireless, she could have run for the rest of her life.

This was existential, shifting, fragile. On certain days she would suddenly feel heavy again, and find herself sinking through the multiple layers of herself, in a downward spiral towards the bottom of everything thinkable. She'd want to sit down, to lie down and never get up. Her feet met the ground heavy and flat, her breath grew painful, exhaustion gripped her again and wrapped itself over everything she knew. She saw no other way but to give up. Existence wore so thin that it tore. She had believed she was strong but found herself weaker than the feeblest fifteen-year-old running through the park for the very first time. She wanted to lie down and die. But she didn't, she wasn't one to die, not like that, not yet; she ran through the nausea, through the self-loathing, the despair and exhaustion. She touched on the thinnest stratum of her being, the very weakest, which nobody else knew about, which even she did not want to know about.

The thinnest stratum of her instinct to survive, she thought to herself. Although the word instinct implied an absence of conscious decision. Perhaps the will to survive, the will to hold out, was a more precise description. Perhaps what she had reached, as so many others before, was her will's last membrane before the abyss, where we can no longer help ourselves? Taut and transparent, like a thinly worn layer of fat stretched over bare bone, like the skin of a drum, a little white drum that no one likes to hear? But something struck that drum, rubbed against that membrane, far below the surface of her life, beneath everything that had become her.

She ran, and she felt something beating repeatedly on a thin, tightly stretched, translucent membrane, and from there she sank no further. From there she would build herself up. She ran in the morning before work. She ran before anyone else was out of bed. She created herself, she built herself up fibre by fibre, she built muscles and determination and the ability to hold out and survive whatever happened. For anything can happen, anything can happen at any moment, in anyone's life. It's a fact.

4

ONCE, LONG AGO, SHE HAD DECIDED WHO SHE
would be. It had happened early in her life, and she could
still feel it in her body for years afterwards, a decision that
fixed itself deep in her flesh like a preserving salt. The
decision that she would manage, survive. She would be a
person that others could lean on.

When she was twelve or thirteen, someone had
described her as 'solid'. A slightly odd word rarely used
now, but the dictionary (she liked dictionaries) offered a
meaning that approximated her own understanding of it:
reliable, sober-minded, practical, of sound principle. She
wanted to be all those things. She wanted to be someone
on whom others could count. She wanted to help, never
to need help. Her voice should be heard in a room, loud
and clear, sincere and totally Norwegian. She would manage for herself. And manage for others too. It wasn't difficult, just a matter of deciding. Her face was shaped by
that decision. Her eyes grew large and scrutinising. Her
lips closed gently above a neat chin. There was a naked
candour about her long, pale neck. And the way she turned
her head. Her back too was long and graceful; she'd often
heard that, at least from me.

She was slim, quite short, and often looked rather too
skinny and lightweight. This annoyed her, it made her

overly feminine, she thought, sweet and harmless. This troubled her from an early age, she'd have preferred to be strong. She'd gone to the gym, lifted weights and worked to build her muscles. Her hands gained a firmness and became more defined in a way that pleased her, as did her upper arms. And then she'd taken up running. She had started to be the person she'd always wanted to be; grown-up and strong, a success professionally. And then she met him.

His first name was Gunnar. Eventually I'd call him Gloveman. In those first few weeks after meeting him, she called him by his full name, Gunnar Gunnarsson, whenever she mentioned him, to distinguish him from another Gunnar we knew, from a family whose kids were the same age as ours. She'd tell me that Gunnar Gunnarsson had sent her a text, that Gunnar Gunnarsson had asked if she wanted to come for a run, or that she'd arranged with Gunnar Gunnarsson to go to the climbing centre. She stopped using his surname eventually, the inflection of her voice was enough for it to be clear who she meant. At first I followed suit, and also referred to him as Gunnar whenever we talked about him, and I enunciated his name with teasing intimacy. It was a kind of joke between us, we made his presence into something we shared, something that involved us both. But then, when it started to get difficult for me, I no longer wanted his name on my tongue. (Typical of me to formulate it like that, not wanting his name *on my tongue*, I sexualised my jealousy to make it easier for myself, and perhaps for her too, but it bothered her more than she could find words for.)

He'd given her a pair of cycling gloves, soft, black gloves that only reached the middle joint of the fingers leaving the tips exposed. Small oval holes at the knuckles and an oblong opening on the back of the hand, giving them a carefully crafted, exclusive appearance. They were undoubtedly expensive. But more importantly they were practical, the kind of gift she loved to receive, no matter from whom. (The joy she got from such little gifts – how had he guessed that?) That they were from him gave them special significance. They marked an unspoken, yet obvious shift in their relationship. This gift was a clear invitation that she could neither refuse nor leave without a response. She received them from him one morning just as they were setting off on a long bike ride together, which was to last from early in the morning until late at night. They'd both taken time off from work, going midweek so as not to impact on family time. I was perhaps alone in knowing they were going, she still shared all their conversations with me, but she wasn't sure he was equally open at home. She suspected he kept their friendship a secret, and she liked that. But the gloves were a problem. On her return home that night, she shoved them into her pocket, before wheeling her bicycle through the gate. Then when she'd carried it down to the basement, she was careful to leave the gloves down there too. The following day she brought them up, cramming them hastily into her bag so I wouldn't see them, keen to keep their existence to herself. She didn't notice that she'd dropped one on the stairs. It lay there until I found it. I asked if it was hers. Her face went red. She regretted it later, it would have been so easy to say she'd bought them herself. But everything had always been so open between us, right from the start, and she'd only tried to hide them because she didn't want to start lying.

After that I began calling him Gloveman. A nickname that upset her, on his behalf, when she first heard it. But when I'd said it a few times it took on a different feel, it sounded softer, somehow affectionate and even deferential, as though Gloveman's entrance into her life was something in which I was not only involved, but also found a certain submissive pleasure. I would put my hand on her arm and say:

– Are you going out with Gloveman tonight? Or do you fancy doing something with me?

Hearing me say it nearly always gave her little shock, a shudder of excitement that she felt sure I shared. We'd been together so long and become so entwined, that we could share everything and anything – or so we believed.

How did the two of us get together? Once I'd been a young father, I had a young child in my arms, she leaned forward to talk to this child before looking at me. She was a medical student, studying to be a doctor, and was on a clinical placement at the surgery where I'd taken my daughter. She was sitting in my GP's consulting room. She called us in from the waiting room, greeting us as we came in, my child first, and then me. My daughter sat on my lap and smiled shyly at the grown-up lady, who was actually still a very young woman, a few years my junior. My daughter must have noticed that I felt relaxed, that I leaned back in my chair. She released my hand and stretched out across the table to investigate something that was being shown to her. A worn-out plastic toy, a yellow duck, or no, a red sausage dog. The sort of object you might find in any GP surgery that welcomes small children. It made a thin, ingratiating squeak when you squeezed it. She remembers my daughter's hands clutching this red dog. Of course, it is me who remembers it. But we talked about it so often, during all those conversations when we analysed our first meeting, it became a shared memory. My daughter was small, she knew nothing of the adult world, it was easy for her to trust a stranger. And I, her father, also put my trust in the woman who sat opposite. I gave more than trust, I gave myself, without thought, holding nothing back, I had already seen something in her, or opened myself to the possibility of seeing something that I wasn't meant to see, that was the feeling. But what happened? Was it just that our gazes met, and that we held them a little longer than we ought? Did something happen between us without our either wanting or knowing it? Or was I already on the lookout for someone? And did she become that someone just because she was nice enough to talk to my child? Was it because her eyes were so large and empathic, because her voice was so gentle when she spoke to my child? I remember the easy weight of my daughter on my lap, how safely, comfortably and heavily she sat there. The dog had long black ears, my daughter's hands were fat and chubby, and always slightly moist.

And Timmy's adult hands, strong, with short nails. She stroked the little girl's cheek and asked her to *open very wide.* And she did. My daughter opened her mouth, a plastic dog in her hands, she felt completely safe, ready to do anything she was asked, and Timmy leaned forward and stared into that little gaping mouth. Her tonsils were swollen, that was obvious. There was medicine for that, and Timmy could write a prescription. Or perhaps she couldn't, not formally, it would be another two years before she was fully qualified. But for me it felt as though she took charge of my child, and simultaneously took charge of me. She'd made us both feel safe. She was secure in herself and in the world, and I felt secure in her presence.

Such encounters, fleeting and completely open, happen all the time. All of us meet people we could fall in love with, everywhere and anywhere. Quite unexpectedly you look into the face of someone who looks earnestly and searchingly back at you. A person who has something you'd like to possess, an attitude, confidence, playfulness. It rarely comes to anything; perhaps you're already in a relationship, and he or she is also in a relationship, and you both move on. Most of these encounters are forgotten because they lead to nothing. You pass someone you might have married as you board the bus, your glances meet, but you never see each other again. And as you get off the bus you pass another person with whom you could also have lived quite happily. One of you gives a tentative smile, the other smiles back, but it's too late. Everywhere there are people who might have found each other, but don't. If all of these people reached out to each other, few marriages would last more than a day, a week or a month – or perhaps a couple of years if they were helplessly happy. Incidentally, there is probably always something helpless about happiness, in devoting oneself to another.

But she was in a relationship already. And it was obvious, she thought, that I was too, I was unlikely to be alone with such a young child, few men are. We shook hands, somewhat formally, and looked into each other's eyes, smiling lightly, and for just a fraction longer than necessary. Then I left with my daughter in my arms, but as we reached the corridor, my eye caught hers again. She hadn't counted on that, it did something to her, I seemed so safe, warm and vibrantly alive to her, she didn't know that she was the cause of this security, warmth and vibrancy, she didn't recognise her own confidence when it was reflected so strongly back to her.

A closeness, a calm, a potential tenderness.

She liked to be near me because I liked to be near her. She watched as I carefully shut the door of the office where she sat. She heard our voices out in the corridor. The baby-voice was suddenly loud and clear, liberated from all shyness. She heard my daughter say that *the lady was very kind*, and she heard the young father's self-assured voice answer. He was, she understood, in agreement.

That was all, it lasted no longer. My daughter was her very first patient. Later, neither of us could remember whether my own GP was present, she must have been, but in our story of that first meeting nobody else is present apart from my child. A few minutes' sympathetic and friendly exchange. Under normal circumstances we'd have forgotten each other afterwards. Timmy was still a student, so was I, and in addition I was, or rather wanted to be, a writer. I had ambitions to be a journalist, somebody who wrote in-depth articles on a wide variety of topics. Most of all I wanted be a science journalist, so I regularly followed lectures outside my own discipline. That was how we met again. We attended the same lecture series, probably on social medicine, it was a main area of interest for her. And I was interested in most things, so it seemed, and she recognised me instantly.

Or, not quite. She recognised me, but couldn't remember where from. I was looking at everyone, I turned unabashed to all and sundry, as if everyone held secrets into which I longed to be initiated, as though everyone apart from me knew how life should be lived. I had one of those faces, wide-eyed, wide-mouthed, always alert and interested. She walked past me during a break and said hi, and I said hi back, rather vaguely, since I couldn't place her either. But I smiled and she saw I looked pleased, as though I associated her with something nice. Suddenly she remembered where she knew me from, and in that instant I remembered too, and we immediately started talking.

It was a long conversation that lasted nearly twenty years. In the beginning I used to stand and wait for her before or after lectures. I was the man she had entered into conversation with, the man with the crumpled shirts, the man with a worn-out jacket with the seams torn at the cuffs and threads dangling over his hands. A certain unkempt look that appealed to her perhaps. But I was also a person who expressed interest in her and in what she knew, in what she was studying. I'd listen as she explained the world for herself and for me. She recognised my smile and scrawny shoulders from far away, head lifted, neck stretched long, afraid of missing anything. I'd wait for her, she'd walk over to me and we'd leave together.

We started arranging to meet. We took long walks, wandered the streets. I was married, I had a small child, and yet I wanted to spend all my time with Timmy. I frequently had the pushchair, and it was on one of these days that she first sang to my daughter. A lullaby she'd learned from her father, about a little boy who sat on a mountaintop and played a horn, a ram's horn. After we moved in together she always sang it for my daughter, and later she sang it for our two sons, up through the years, until suddenly she no longer sang it, at least not that I heard.

She told me about her background, where she came from, what kind of child she'd been. I did the same. I talked about trees and birds, talked about meaning, about life, and how I wanted life to be. She told me about her studies. We talked about the kind of food we liked to make, shared our thoughts on politics and sex and how children should be brought up. We were driven, purposeful, something inside us knew what we both wanted with each other long before we acknowledged it ourselves. My daughter started to recognise her.

One morning we were out together; she had a break from lectures, I was looking after my daughter. I was pushing the buggy and she was walking beside me while my daughter slept. We sat on a bench. I turned to her. She knew what I would say before I said it. She had known it would come, while not really knowing, but she had no doubt as soon as I began.

– Imagine if the two of us could be friends.

– We can, we already are.

– I mean very good friends.

– That's what I mean too.

Something in my face altered, I moved too close and she had to look away, but I said:

– I mean more than friends. I'm in love with you.

She was in her mid-twenties, I was a little over thirty, our lives were just beginning. She was about to qualify as a doctor, I had recently started out as a journalist, freelancing for some weekly newspapers, hoping for something permanent. We both came from families in which nobody had ever gone on to higher education. Our families had been made up of smallholders and fishermen, sailors and artisans, lowly office workers and unskilled factory labourers. She and I were the products of a rise in living standards for all, and we went off to university with a blissfully unaware sense of entitlement, which only decades of prosperity in Norway had made possible. But early in our schooldays we had embarked on another education, a training for careers in love, courtship, cohabitation, the devotion to another that would supposedly make it possible to hold out against all else. She started finding herself boyfriends at thirteen, I began with girls a bit later. By the time we met we had each had a series of partners and we had both lived with people, I'd even had a child and got married. Now, these relationships were revealed to us as nothing but a preliminary exercise for this unique moment. We had, at long last, found each other. We reached out to each other, we put our arms around each other, our faces drew close, we opened our mouths, and kissed. I stuck my tongue in her mouth, she was taken aback, it happened so suddenly, but then she met my tongue with hers. There followed uninterrupted kissing with tongues for a full minute or more, then we pulled our faces apart and stared at each other with fresh eyes. We were finally an 'us'.

She thinks she can recall our voices, they must have been gentle, open. Voices reflect each other's pitch, and we talked on together, very softly, softer than we'd talk to anyone else. It sounded warm and slightly childlike, light and intimate. We found a tone and volume which we made our own, which we shared with nobody else. We sat on that bench for a long time, kissing and embracing. She felt my hands under her clothes. I was moving fast, she'd not experienced that before, already after that first kiss I was stroking her stomach, touching her bare skin.

My daughter woke up. She was lying in her buggy with a blanket over the hood to keep out the light. Now she pulled it down, and lay there looking at us. Her gaze as open and assured as only a child's can be. She was two years old, with a pale, round, sleepy face; she sat up and said:

– What are you *doing*, Daddy?

Timmy remembers that now, it comes to her one evening when she's out for a walk, she's not thought of it for years, but suddenly she recalls the two-year-old's voice, breathy and crackly with sleep. That little voice that burst so softly, so innocently in on the life we had already started to build together.

So we became a couple. I went home, ended it with the child's mother, the woman I'd married just a couple of years earlier. She, the mother of my child, soon to be the woman-I-was-once-married-to. She'd been such a young mother, and I'd called her my Sweetgrass, though later I called her Sad Honeydew, and then she became Blind Thistle. But she never knew of these other names, I never said them aloud. Though she must have noticed the shift. One day there were three, me and her and our baby, there was never meant to be anyone else, another child perhaps, that might have come – *would* have come if we'd stayed together. She was a musician, played the guitar and sang, wrote her own songs. She'd started to make a living from it, just about. A time would come when she'd make a reasonably decent living from it, but I was out of her life by then. Later still, she began teaching, though by then she'd given up playing long ago. And our daughter had finally grown up, and was no longer dragged between two parents who didn't speak to each other.

It was a Thursday in May. Something caused my Sweetgrass to change for me into Sad Honeydew and eventually into Blind Thistle. She was sitting there with her guitar, she could spend the whole day playing a single chord, or so it seemed. When I came in, she looked up at me with one eye shut, as she always did, a problem in one of her pupils caused her to squint at the world one-eyed, as

though the light were too strong. All her life she had prepared herself for bad news, for personal catastrophe, but
not from me. I was the man who would always be there,
holding out with her, the man who would make it possible for her to get up in the morning, to get dressed and
brush her hair and apply an uneven line of lipstick before
going out. I was the father of her child. The father of a
miracle which made me even more precious to her than
before. It was the three of us now. We would take care of
our child and of each other whenever the world started to
rock. Which the world frequently did, for us both, for no
apparent reason.

But now I came home with our child in my arms saying that I no longer wanted to be with her. It didn't make
sense. Surely I couldn't stand there with our child in my
arms and say it was over. It couldn't be over, we were bound
together through living flesh. And yet I came home to her
and said *I have to talk to you*, in a voice that boded death
and catastrophe.

Or did I? Was that just how Timmy imagined it all later
– the woman who was my new girlfriend before I'd even
finished with the previous one? After the kiss, Timmy
and I met every day. We took walks and sat on benches.
One day we sat in the park, talking about the things new
lovers talk about: trees, childhood, what to do for sensi-
tive skin, movies, and the origins of language. We were
tentative and unsure, since we didn't know each other,
though we had decided that we knew each other better
than anyone else ever could; besides, our bodies were
drawn to each other, and thus we achieved a closeness

which seemed to eclipse all else. Then my daughter woke up and I headed slowly home with her, Timmy accompanying me part of the way. And then by some grotesque coincidence the woman to whom I was still married ran into us there in the street. I was pushing the buggy, our child's pale, trusting face gazing up at me, at the two of us, at the trees and the houses and sky. And there right beside me was Timmy, to whom I'd now promised myself, holding my arm, just as the child's mother had done only days before. She watched us walking together with the pushchair, talking and laughing. We didn't notice her before she came running towards us, took the buggy and screamed at me.

Look now, at these two who have fallen so suddenly and helplessly in love. A very young woman and a very young father. Look at the young mother who is in the midst of being abandoned by her young husband, watch how she grabs the buggy and runs off with it. She has suffered the grossest betrayal, and now she has nothing left but her child. She will not let go of that. The child lies there in its buggy, aware of nothing.

That was the start of the divorce which Timmy heard about only through me. The angry attempts at conversation between two people who had been lovers but who would be lovers no longer. We were meant to tear ourselves free from each other now, each obliged to describe our pain to the other, to discuss the betrayal and disappointment, and the reasons for that betrayal and disappointment, when in truth neither of us had any idea what those reasons were.

The abandoned person becomes helplessly bound to the person who abandons. She hasn't chosen this. She screams at me, berates me, cries silent, bitter tears. She can't sleep, can't sit still. She thinks she wants to die. Or rather, she wants to live, but only together with me. She rings my new girlfriend, and yells at her down the phone. She rings everybody she knows, talks to everybody, day and night, tries to talk her way to some understanding of what's happened, of how everything could change so abruptly and without warning. She gets no help from me. I don't want to talk, I don't dare to, can't bear to. I've made my decision, all I want is to get away from the life that I've lived, the life I've suddenly realised I couldn't hold out with. I don't think I need to explain myself. I've already promised myself to another, and this new-found love, look, how it erases everything else. Or nearly everything, not my child, though I renounce the possibility of seeing her every day. I tell everybody, myself included, that there is no other solution. I choose this new love, and with that I walk away from everything that has been.

Anybody who wants to can find reasons as to why a young married couple might not manage to stay together. We were too different or too alike. We were too close or not close enough. Too young to know ourselves or each other. We were oversensitive, in our different ways, and insensitive to each other's sensitivities. The woman whom I had secretly begun to call Blind Thistle talks to everybody she knows, and they all try to help her by explaining how it could happen. But I'm the only one placed to give her any explanation, and I don't know what to say. I've just met someone else, and now I'd rather have her, the other.

It was that easy and that sudden, as a thin-worn rope that snaps. But, of course, there wasn't any rope, nor was it even worn out. There must have been a tenderness between us, intimacy, trust. There must have been a loving union of two bodies. Loyalty and the promise of a shared future. And yet it was over in a flash, and then it was as though our intimacy and trust, this loving union, had never existed at all. For how can we conceive a loving union that doesn't last? Can there ever have been a true union, if it doesn't last?

One day, she – the woman who had been so thoughtlessly betrayed – rang me and said:

– I just want to say one thing.

– Surely there's nothing more to be said.

– Oh yes. There's more to say than you can imagine. But you don't want to listen, and I've given up. So I'll just say one last thing, and it's this: I hope you'll experience this yourself one day. I hope with all my heart that you'll be left in the same way as you've left me.

That was the last thing she said. Not the last, of course, but the last that would reverberate between her and me. Years later I could still recall those words and the voice that delivered them, aggressive, tormented, bewildered, a mix of trembling breath and crackling fury, and I could still hear her gasp, gathering whatever air she could muster to launch carefully judged volleys of sound to strike me down. A sort of threat, I believed, a promise she could not fulfil herself, but which she hoped another would carry through. And I did experience it, I was abandoned, I lost the only person I trusted, just as she had done. I too would stand there and be that person who was no longer wanted. That was what she wished for me, and it wasn't hard to understand why, not even for me.

I pushed what she'd said away from me, told myself I had no use of it. But I never forgot it. It came back, frequently, long after she and I ceased to know each other. And a song she'd once sung echoed in my head when I woke up at half past four in the morning. *Further on up the road*, it warned. Just wait, it said. Someone will hurt you, just as you've hurt me. You think you'll get away with it, but it's waiting for you. That was what she wished for, that was what she wanted to say. *Further on up the road*. Those were the words I'd hear her sing in my head long after she and I had stopped talking. But I didn't want to listen to that song. Why would I?

Timmy wasn't obliged to deal with all this. She split up with her boyfriend. It was easier. Although, who can actually say that it's ever easy to leave somebody? It was difficult, almost unbearable, it always is, for anybody, but it passed. He cried, they both cried, they had a few painful conversations, and then it was over.

Once, Timmy had made a decision about who she was going to be. She would manage for herself, and she would manage for others, and never need help. At night, when she still slept alone, she'd sometimes wake up and think about who she was and who she might become. We'd got together and life would now begin, *our* life, the life that would spread itself to cover over everything we'd done before. Every night we lay in bed, naked and eager, as though we'd never been naked with anyone else before.

We moved in together, first into one apartment, then into a bigger one, and later into a third which was even bigger. We bought a bed for ourselves and a bed for my daughter, and later we bought beds for the children we had together. We bought chairs and tables, hung pictures and laid carpets and drove the car. We built an existence, acquired habits, it went of its own accord. We wrote our names on our mailboxes and front doors, one name beneath the other. We were a unit. We heard and understood as a unit, overheard and misunderstood, blinded ourselves in unison, imitated each other's good sides. We took from each other and whatever the world could give us with bold optimism. Our debts increased, but the bank had a new policy, good customers no longer needed to clear the loan itself, just pay the interest. Our debts would never decrease, we only paid the banks what it cost them to lend us the money. We might pay off our debts later, or perhaps never, things would just roll on, average earnings increased a little every year, and so would ours, the economy could only get stronger, our existence too, the love, the joy, the despair, everything, could only grow in strength. We went out together in the mornings, came home at night, sat at the table, walked across floors, lay in our beds. Our voices would sound in these rooms forever.

There was just *one* thing that must never happen. I'd think about it now and then, not often, but during all

49

those years we lived together, it went through me like a cold ravine, ten or perhaps twenty times, and each time it was crippling, as though we were threatened by a major disaster. *Further on up the road. I was going to get hurt too.* And on those rare but poignant occasions, when I had to make a wish, one of those wishes that I didn't believe in, but took very seriously – like when one of the kids and I said the same word simultaneously, and I had to link little fingers with them and make a wish never to be told – then I'd wish that Timmy and I would stay together forever and that nobody would ever come between us. So perhaps I did fear it after all? Fear it more than anything else? I kept it to myself, and more, I kept it hidden from myself, only letting it out in these playfully loaded occasions.

I lived as though my life took place only before her eyes. She was rather startled when I said this. It was me she woke with and slept with, it was me she had all those long conversations with, until the day she no longer did. I would come home in the afternoon from some job or other, I only had short assignments with the smaller papers in those first years. I'd write in the office, then come home and continue writing until late. There was always some article I couldn't get finished, something I couldn't get right, something I had to try to improve. I often got up in the middle of the night to work while she and the kids were asleep. I'd wake her in the morning having been up for hours. She'd be woken by me lying down beside her, or on top of her. She woke to the sound of my voice, talking about us, about her, about the love we shared that I couldn't manage without.

Outwardly our life changed: we had children, first one little boy and then another. Two boys born five years apart. She started work as a GP at a health centre, and I got a permanent job with a major newspaper. So I was finally what I'd always hoped to be, a journalist on an editorial team. I had my own desk and my own computer, went to early-morning meetings with other journalists and editors. On the face of it, everything was perfect. I wrote articles that were widely read and that got me recognition in certain circles. I was made section editor, and did well at it. But something wasn't quite right with the job, or with the role that I felt forced to assume as a journalist. For a while I'd leave home dressed in a smart dark suit; not because anyone at work demanded it, but because, as I explained to her, I needed some sort of protection. I took it off the minute I got home in the evening, stripping off my work attire to become myself again. And then, just as I was starting my paternity leave to be with our second boy, the newspaper industry went into meltdown. My colleagues began taking jobs as researchers and media consultants. Like many others I was offered a redundancy package, I accepted, and I was a freelancer once more. I extended my time at home with our youngest, we didn't apply for a nursery place for him until he was three, and even then I continued to stay at home. I wrote a children's book that got published with a degree of success, I wrote another, and soon Timmy and the kids were used to my being at home, and my sitting there writing.

It occurs to Timmy that something changed around this time. Whenever she got back from work, there I was, without fail, with the kids. And the home to which she returned was not as before, its rooms had become an extension of my inner life. There we were, the children and I, waiting. I'd always have made dinner and have cleaned and tidied everything with a fastidiousness she could never get used to. But more than this, I was also getting increasingly obsessed with her. Perhaps I simply had too much time to think, now that I spent so much time alone. I told her how I could sit all day wondering how the kids were at school, mulling over what she or I had said or done the day before. She had become even more central to my life than ever before. I wanted to talk to her about every single thing she did and thought. And that was hard for her to understand. And my writing probably had its effect. It seemed to me that I'd grown more vulnerable not only from being alone, but from having a job that allowed me to go into myself. Perhaps that was why a general sensitivity − if one can talk of general sensitivities − took hold in me: I was constantly observing the intricacies of my own emotions, since I used them now in my writing, and with that perhaps she loomed larger in my consciousness, indeed everything that was important to me grew in significance. Still, it confused her. It was flattering to be admired, but she'd always felt more drawn to me when I was scarcely home, when I was too busy to think so much about her.

But I was glad of these days at home, I said, I'd started to find myself. My redundancy had come in the nick of time; had I stayed at the newspaper I'd have lost touch with everything I liked best in myself. She listened, but suggested I was more robust working in a professional setting, with other people. She was keen to offer a counterbalance, an alternative perspective. She'd liked being with me when I was at the paper, when the life I led reflected her own.

Now all I wanted was to hear about everything that happened to her. She worked hard and was beginning to achieve her goals. She had specialised, gone on to gain a doctorate, before taking a job at the Department of Health, where she was made head of the division, responsible for research into public health. We had gone in opposite ways, she told family and friends. She had abandoned her patients – all those unique cases, babies, pensioners, teenage girls with their diagnosed and undiagnosable ailments – because she wanted to work in a wider social capacity, because she wanted to influence the circumstances that affect everyone's lives. Meanwhile, I was at home now, busy writing short stories about children reminiscent of the child I had once been, or might have been: individual stories about special cases, emotional truths, nothing more.

We'd gone through that first phase – that initial flush of love – during which we occasionally had my little daughter, and were a new couple left to our own devices for the rest of the time. Long mornings in bed, devoted to our bodies' pleasure-seeking explorations. Then came the home-building phase with young children, baby food all over the kitchen worktops and tiny clothes drying over the bath. Then the kids got bigger, more voices joined the conversation round the table, and she and I were seldom alone.

Except at night, in bed. There we lived a secret life, about which we spoke to no one, a warm dark tunnel through the days. Out there, up in the light, we did our jobs, socialised with friends who almost without exception had children the same age as ours. We attended parents' groups, went shopping on Fridays, cried when anything got too much, followed the news, discussed the professional issues in our respective fields. Or we drove the kids to their sports activities (Timmy) or took them to the library (me). She began taking regular exercise and I volunteered for an environmental organisation. We had more money and filled the family diary, much like everyone else around us. Afternoons, weekends, holidays: we made plans and carried them out as best we could, packed the car and unpacked it again, screamed at the kids to come down from their rooms and leave their computer games. Our life resembled that of everyone else, superficially at least, which gave us a sense of belonging and calm. But the thing that bound us together, that gave us a sense of continuity, was this secret life that concerned only the two of us, and which we called our love.

It had to be love. What else could it be? And it had to be a great love, an exceptionally great and utterly overwhelming love. There had to be a closeness, a unity and an attraction between us that was far beyond the ordinary. Or it wouldn't have been worth it, worth the separation from my daughter, which meant I only saw her once a fortnight – and not even that, in those first few years. My daughter was two years old when I fell in love with Timmy. How could I justify this betrayal to myself, or to my daughter when she grew up, if this upheaval in our lives hadn't been caused by a uniquely great and earth-shattering love?

We didn't have any mutual friends when we first got together. New couples often don't. My old friends had to choose whether or not to accept the fact I'd left my wife because I'd fallen in love with someone else. The same went for Timmy's old friends. We were met with scepticism from both sides. How could they not think that we'd let some random flirtation destroy the lives we already had? Who hasn't heard of men – particularly men – or women who fall head over heels in love and destroy what they have, only to discover later that their new relationship is a mistake, a moment of blind sexual infatuation? Such romances rarely lead to long-term relationships. I was a thirty-year-old dad who'd fallen in love with the young doctor who treated his daughter for a sore throat. Timmy was the young doctor who'd fallen for the father of a little girl in her care. Before even qualifying, she'd broken one of the unwritten cardinal rules in patient treatment. How could anyone believe that what we had would last?

We lay in bed together, naked and sweaty, the room smelling of sex, talking about our future life together. Telling each other that all this would make a good story some day. Right now 'we' were a bad story, right now 'we' were regarded as nothing but a careless springtime affair that had wrecked everything for our previous partners, for my child and both our families. Only we had faith in the two of us. But we took the task seriously. 'We' were a bad story that would almost imperceptibly turn into a good story, as the years passed and our love appeared to be the sole love ever to have existed in our lives, for the kids at least, and eventually everyone else. No other love was thinkable, we were the perfect match, it seemed after time. Is it possible, in fact, to live with someone for decades without believing that he or she is the only one? We knew there were other possible lives, other possible lovers, perhaps better lives and better lovers, even for us. But we did not want, we could not allow, this thing that we'd built up to fall apart, we didn't want to leave each other because of some random 'falling-in-love', as we had done before so as to be together. On that we were agreed. We could not do to each other what we had done to our previous partners.

Yet it was essential that we set each other free. After all, we had liberated desire in each other, together we had unleashed our curiosity and zest for life. We mustn't guard each other and restrict each other's freedom. We didn't want to live under some sort of apartheid, she with her girlfriends and me with some buddy or other. We wanted to live together, not in segregated male and female worlds. We wanted to be each other's confidants, to share the best and most intimate conversations with each other, not with some random friends. And we succeeded in this. We succeeded until our pact led her to confide something in me that she ought to have kept to herself. If I hadn't been privy to every single exchange she had with Gloveman, as I called him, what then? Then it might have been a flirtation that was allowed to develop quietly, in secret, and that could have ended equally secretly.

But there must have been a trigger for the events that drove us apart. Perhaps they were already set in motion at the very start. During that first summer we took a holiday to a foreign city. We wandered through streets, unable to keep our hands off each other. We lay in a bed together naked. All night and for much of the day we lay in that bed calling forth pleasure in each other. We sat at a table, our hands seeking each other, meeting between cups and glasses and plates. Our feet found each other too, on the floor beneath. Even the tips of our shoes sought each other. She kicked off one shoe and stroked my leg with her toes. She didn't like her feet much, not back then, she thought they were too big and coarse, with stubby toes and thick nails, but she liked using them like hands, she was good at that. She was good at picking things up from the floor with her toes, and liked pinching me with them. She shoved her bare foot between my legs. She felt it do something to me. She noticed red blotches spread across my neck. We got up to leave, to return to the bed, to the hotel room, but we needed to pay first. We stood together at the till, and a young man came over to help, to take the money. She looked at him, she froze, everything seemed to go a fraction slower, she seemed almost to linger as she moved through the sudden sweetness of attraction. The young man behind the counter noticed nothing, making him even more attractive.

But she didn't know it herself. She wasn't aware of it until later, when I started to talk about it. Desire does not see itself. She had blinded herself to her own gaze, she couldn't even remember looking at him afterwards. She must have taken him in, registered his presence through her own living, sensate body, this body that continually absorbed impressions, openly and non-defensively, as bodies do. It lasted only a few seconds, but I was in love, I searched her whole being with my gaze, I observed how directed she became, and saw that she blinded herself. She had blinded herself for my sake, I told her. And she could go blindly from me to another. I was the man she loved, in my arms she grew soft and loving, yet she had had lingered, blind under his gaze — a totally random guy.

Without giving it a thought herself. Until I mentioned it. And then she remembered that she had noticed something about him, something she liked. Who wouldn't be attracted to a tall young man? A man with beautiful hands, tall and lanky, sensuous but gauche, touched by shyness perhaps, or youth, or something else. His heavy yet aimless desire may not have been focused on her, yet she felt it, and immediately she came within touching distance, something in her changed. As though her attention was caught, as though she listened, sniffed the air, homed in on him.

But it lasted only a moment. It flashed through her, and she didn't notice it herself, not until later. And even if she had noticed it, she would probably have forgotten it. Random desire flashes through us all, sniffs at everything, changes its mind and shifts direction. Bodies turn to each other, bodies turn from each other again. It happens, there's nothing more to it, we don't even think about it, we forget it again. She was simply open, she simply let herself be charmed, she was simply alive. And I was open to everything that happened in her. I didn't need to observe this. And having observed it, I had no need to talk about it. I could have pushed it aside and left her in peace. It was her moment, she was the one who was touched, or whatever she might call it. It had merely been a kind of light arousal, fleeting.

So couldn't I have just let it lie? she thought later.

Clearly not.

When we came back out into the street that summer's day, she felt my hand on the small of her back. A light touch, my voice light and warm too, asking

– did you like him?

and she said

– who?

and I said

– that man in there,

and she looked at me, my face was still blotchy with love and curiosity. I seemed so relaxed and happy, I wasn't fearful, and so neither was she. She felt relaxed and happy too, there was no danger, we were just having fun, and she said

– Well, he was rather nice.

– I could tell you thought that.

– You could?

I was her boyfriend, we were together, she'd thought it had finally begun, the life that was to be hers. She was going to live that life with me. And there I stood, holding her hand and saying she'd looked at another man, or boy. That I'd witnessed her tense up when she saw him. And that it was obvious. Obvious she liked him. She felt my hand on her hip now. A warm hand, that moved up to her

59

waist. She felt me pull her to me. My face drew very close, I whispered in her ear, I said

– I could see you wanted him,

and she grew uneasy and thought *what happens now?* and then a second later her fear subsided. She recalled that it had happened, she had felt his gaze on her and then a heat in her belly, or perhaps lower. And then she'd forgotten it, unaware that I'd seen it. She ought to be more careful perhaps to ensure it didn't happen again. But no, she needn't be. It posed no danger, it may even be a good thing. I stood there whispering into her ear, warmth in my voice, and I said

– What was it you liked about him?

and then she told me, without reflection. As though talking to herself, perhaps, and she said

– He had nice hands. He was tall, a long lean body. And his eyes. He looked at me with a kind of smile in his eyes, and then I wanted him. But it was only like a flicker, for a second. I'd forgotten it when you mentioned it,

and I said

– But you remember it now?

and she said

– Yes, but I didn't realise you could see it,

and we walked back to the hotel, walked quickly through the warm summer streets, our arms around each other to make each other safe, and to feel our bodies move against each other. And because that's what couples do. And there, as we walked through the old quarter, with its bridges and towers, I went on talking about what I'd observed. About how she'd opened up to another man, a man who just happened to be there. She listened as I went on about it. Heard me say it created a burning inside me, that it made me feel alive. I often said things like that. She didn't quite understand what I meant. She asked me to explain. I said that I saw her more distinctly somehow when I saw her looking at somebody else. I liked talking about it, clearly, it did something to me, she saw that. And so it did something to her too.

– I liked seeing you open up to him.

– I don't think he noticed.

– I'd say these things are always noticeable. Wouldn't you agree?

– You may be right. It's an exciting idea.

– He looked at you and wanted you. And it turned you on.

– Could you see that?

– Yes, I saw that it did something to you.

– But what?

– It made you wet, maybe.

– Oh, I don't think so. Did you think that? That I got wet?

– I'm certain you did.

– You'll soon find out for yourself.

We walked into the hotel and stood together in the little lift. We stared into each other's eyes. I placed my hand on her hip. Pulled her to me and looked into her face. She was under my gaze. She was aware of being seen by me. Seen, she thought, as she'd never been seen by anyone before. It was a turn-on and slightly frightening. We went down the corridor and found the door to our room and let ourselves in. I began to take her clothes off. She was wearing a dress, no, not a dress, not that day, it was a green T-shirt with a picture of a yellow hand-print on it, and white dungarees and white socks and shoes. Underneath she had a plain white bra and plain white knickers, and I removed each garment. She usually preferred to do it herself, liking to turn slightly away as she removed her top garments. But now she let me undress her entirely. She remembers only what she wore, not what I wore, despite the fact she probably removed my clothes at the same time as I removed hers. No, that's wrong. She watched as I took off my clothes. I was tall and thin and paler than any other man she'd known. And there was so much I wanted to do with her. My gaze never left her, following her like a torch, searching for life in a vast and incomprehensible darkness.

She doesn't recall this. For years it is forgotten, gone. Then one night it comes back to her. How we lay in that bed, lovers for no more than six months, and I whispered in her ear about all the thrilling things she could do with another man. Who would say such things? Almost nobody, we thought. But I said them. And now I'd begun, I couldn't stop. And she liked it, it did something to her that she liked.

This stopped for years, then I began doing it again: I lay beside her and whispered softly into her ear about the things another man could do to her. She listened to my voice, she touched herself, and then I penetrated her and everything rushed through her, rising and falling inside her, the imagined and the actual, the man who was actually fucking her and another who might have, as though she lay surrounded by naked men who desired her, only her. She heard herself scream. She heard her voice in that dark room, a single solitary moaning voice. It rose towards the ceiling as though she were calling for herself.

5

– IT'S AMAZING WE MET.

   – That we got together.

   – Incredible really.

   – When we're so different.

   – And now, I could never be with anyone but you.

   – Nor me. Do you think it's like that for everyone?

   – No, I think we're lucky.

   – But to be together with someone means believing that there could never have been anyone else, that there'll always be an *us*, that life could never have been better than this. Did you believe that last time too?

   – No. And I spent the whole time wondering if that was how it was meant to be. If I'd always have doubts. If I'd always wonder whether this was all there was. Perhaps it will never get any better, I thought, perhaps I just have to get used to it. I was constantly in doubt, I couldn't really hold out, yet I stayed with him.

   – You don't doubt it now?

   – Never.

   – Do you like this?

   – Very much.

   – And do you like it now?

   – Do you never have doubts then?

– No, never.

– Not so hard.

– But I didn't last time either.

– Didn't you?

– It wasn't good for me, it was always difficult. She was always upset or offended about something, and I constantly had to try to make her happy again. Even so, I didn't have any doubts. I believed my life had finally begun. But with you everything is so much better. But imagine if things just get better each time? If things came to an end between us, and you got together with someone else, then you might have an even better time with him.

– With whom?

– With someone else. Somebody you haven't met.

– Would you want that?

– No, never. But I'd still love you even if you found someone else.

– I don't believe that.

– But what would love mean otherwise? If I really love you, then I should want your happiness. And if you have a better time with somebody else, I should still love you just as much, right? I ought to support you if you preferred to be with someone else. And I actually believe I would.

– But, darling.

– Yes?

– Be quiet for a moment.

– I talk too much, I know.

– Don't stop, please. But don't say anything.

6

WHAT IS LOVE? WHAT *IS* LOVE? NO, THAT'S NO good. Firstly the question is much too general. And secondly? She's forgotten. The word points to a feeling or an experience that everybody thinks they know, yet it's too limited, and simultaneously too broad. A word like *love* simply encompasses too much. It occurs to her that anyone wanting to say or write anything must trust that each word points to something definite, clearly delineated, easily identified. But that's never the case, a word always points like an open and undecided hand, its fingers spread in many directions.

Still: what was love for us? Was it co-dependence or mad abandon? Did I render myself dependent on her, bow in her shadow, subjugate myself and rest in the light of her existence? And did she do the same? Were we just drawn to each other, wanting to be close, or did we want to give ourselves away entirely? That was how it was for me, according to her. I wanted to share myself with her, I wanted to escape myself, I couldn't take responsibility for everything inside me, not alone.

She remembers my getting undressed and lying close to her. At that moment I was the loving, love-addicted, love-hungry body beside her, the man who wanted to do or be done to. I was the man who was with her, who rested in the simple fact that she existed. I lived my whole life before that pale face. She remembers me saying it. I stepped inside her, hid myself in her very existence, which became mine too, because I was married to her and had given my whole self to her.

That was the phrase I used. Not at the start, not in those first years, but when I started to stay at home, when I became the man who waited for her, who was forever ready to listen to her, to live through her.

She remembers my being at home, that I always preferred to be there. I moved from room to room, cleaning, vacuuming, washing the kids' clothes, her clothes and mine, hanging out the laundry when it was good drying weather, she'd watch me go out with the huge white sheets, bras, T-shirts. Watched me as I stood there hanging them out, reaching up to fasten each garment with small pegs, careful to straighten them on the line so they wouldn't crease. When they were dry, I'd take them down and go inside to fold them neatly. I enjoyed going about like some kind of 1960s housewife, it allowed me to escape myself. She called me *wifey*. She called me *our little wifey*, she knew I liked it, and she began to like it too. Once when I went away, she said, *What will happen to me now? I won't manage without you, without help, we need another wifey.* And I smiled happily back at her, she remembers that smile. She remembers how I liked the smell of laundry that had been dried outside. She thinks of me, not often, but long after she and I no longer know each other, she recalls me sitting quietly in a chair just watching her. She recalls my making risotto with fried beetroot, standing at the kitchen window, preparing supper, listening to music. She gets up and walks into another room, finds something to do, and forgets everything that ever was.

She remembers that whenever I wasn't home I'd always be on my way. I would come home, open the front door and say *I'm back*. Home at last. I'd travelled a whole life-time to come home here. Until then I had been elsewhere, somewhere she wasn't, she couldn't conceive how she'd held out, but now I was there, the man who lived with her. And whenever she wasn't home, I too knew she'd be on her way, that she would be there soon. She remembers this, occasionally she thinks about it, and then remembers it no longer.

But wasn't love also about availing oneself of another's body, another's sweet tenderness and fierce hunger? And oughtn't the other to avail themselves of your body, your tenderness, hunger, despair, joy? Wasn't it about making yourself available, allowing yourself to be undressed, to be touched, to be gazed upon and seen, and in turn about allowing yourself to gaze and see, and to be the one to undress the other?

Yes, and I lay on top of her. I clasped her wrists, quite hard. She liked that, or was it me? Yes, it must have been me who liked it. I needed everything that made us into something other than what seemed ordinary, than what was pre-understood and pre-interpreted, that which left no room for further enquiry. I always wanted something else. I bent her arms up over her head and held both her wrists in one hand. Now she lay with her arms above her head as though she were tied down. My other hand was free to hold her chin, and strike her softly across the cheek. Softly first, then a little harder. She went completely soft when I did that, and let out a sound. She hoped I wouldn't stop, not yet. I pulled her hair, she felt it as I twisted her head to the side. I repositioned her. She felt my hand on her soft round breasts that spilled out so beautifully when she was on her back, she didn't like it herself, but she knew I had a weakness for it. Everything about her made me weak, tender, yielding, adoring, she felt spoiled. I made myself weak for her, it surprised her at first, though later it ceased to surprise her. I surrendered to her entirely. But she liked it most when I wasn't the one to surrender, when I made myself into the one to whom she could surrender. And now, I grabbed her thigh and prised her legs apart. Made her available to me. Thrust myself into her, soon she lay there and let herself be taken, she'd been waiting for that moment. For some time I worried that this made her too feminine, or myself too masculine. I was terrified of being average, ordinary. I didn't want to be a man who just wanted to get his own basic release. There had to be a difference between us and everyone else, she'd often hear me say. She knew this went through my head every time I lay on top of her, every time I thrust myself in and out of her. Was this all there was? I wanted to lie by her side and whisper in her ear until she came. But she'd want me on top of her, and in the end I wanted that too. It was impossible to escape, even for us, that was how we always ended up, with me on top, even though we did just about everything else first, we embraced, tied each other up, hit each other, licked each other, created fantasies for each other and I said *I want you to have everything and everyone, everyone and everything you could ever desire.* It still ended with me lying on top of her and taking her, and with her lying under me, letting herself be taken. Was I just an ordinary man then, and was she just an ordinary woman, after all?

I told her I wanted to see her with someone else. I wanted to see her with more clarity, to see how she was when she wasn't with me. I wanted to see her do the things she couldn't do with me. She said

— Who do you suggest?

and I said

— It has to be someone you like. Maybe we can find him online,

and she said

— No, then we'd have to go for a coffee with him first, I couldn't bear that. Meeting some man who's bought himself a new blue shirt, who's made an effort with himself because he wants to sleep with me, and then having to go back to some strange apartment. That's not for me,

and I said

— Then you'll have to find someone yourself,

and she said

— But what if I fall in love with him?

and I said

— I'm sure we'll survive. It'll be even more exciting, I want to see that you're incapable of resisting him, that it's not me you want, that you don't even think about me being there, and she said

— But won't you be jealous?

and I said

— Yes, probably, that's why it's such a turn-on, I think I like the idea of being pushed aside, being the outsider. It'll just make me love you even more,

and she said

— Let's hope so, though I'm not sure I dare,

and I said

— Oh, I'm sure you do. I know how you look at other men, which is why I can't stop thinking about it. I've got to see it happen, otherwise I'll just be afraid of it, and I don't want to be. I want to see you unbutton his shirt, his trousers, I want to see him step out of his clothes and be naked with you,

and she said

— But afterwards, what do we do then?

— Afterwards I want to kiss him and taste him, I want to lick all the parts that have been inside you. I want you to see me take him in my mouth.

— And what should I do while you're doing this?

— I want you to sit at the other end of the room, I want you to switch off the lamp beside you and pretend that you are watching a film,

then she said

— Come and lie on top of me,

and I did, and there were just the two of us in that room, and for a long time afterwards we lay in silence.

But wasn't this love also an exchange of power? And wasn't the giving of affection, a method of apportioning and distributing tenderness? And didn't this tenderness pre-suppose that one of us took control over the other? Didn't one of us always have to submit to the other, if only for seconds at a time? Yes, yes, that's how it was, I said so, so did she, we both believed it. This applied to any kiss, any embrace, any sexual act: either she was the one who was kissed, embraced, taken, or she was the one who did these things to me. I liked to think we took it in turns, she knew that. And we did, we must have. There must have been an exchange of caring and submission between us, moments or periods when we never quite knew who had taken whose hand, or who received care from whom? Wasn't it like that?

She no longer knows.

But isn't love between two adults also about the fear of liv-ing alone, a desire to escape one's own company at almost any price? Ensuring we have someone to come home to, someone to wait for, someone to care for, to listen to atten-tively, and be gently chided by? Someone's face to look into who perhaps knows who we are or who we are not? Some-one who can say *relax now, come here, lie down beside me.*

Is it just about sharing a bed? Eating together, sitting together, sleeping together, talking together, looking at things together, turning away from the world together? Sleeping together over and over again, lying down naked and waking up in the arms of another who is also naked? And isn't it, at least if you are very lucky – and we were, of course, we believed that – isn't it, most of all, a desire to have uninhibited access to the other? No holds barred. Did we want that? For me she was somebody to take care of, to be loyal to, and also, I said, someone with whom to share even my most twisted thoughts, I liked to talk that way. And for her I was, perhaps, the person who was always there. She no longer knows. But did we really want total and uninhibited access? Wasn't our love in fact rather conventional? A decision to be like others, to replicate the lives of everyone around us, settling down with a spouse and children, and even a garage? To secure access to affection on a permanent basis, company in the evening, sex at night, and a slightly better income?

Yes, that's exactly what it was.

And as a result — and she realises this now — to fail at everything we wanted.

I was the man she'd fallen in love with many years ago. The man with the creased shirts, the pointy nose and an offended look in his eyes. I was the man she'd had children with, who cried when the kids hurt themselves, who was precise about mealtimes, about what we ate, when we ate and where. The man who followed her with his gaze whenever she walked through a room, who was filled with awe just because she existed. She remembers me saying *you can do whatever you want, I'll love you anyway.* And she recalls how the day came when I could no longer say it. That moment came as an amazing relief. Everything blew apart for her, just as she had never imagined it would.

It was a Saturday morning in early June. I was sitting outside on the steps reading, the kids were coming and going, doing their own thing. They generally did, it seems to her, when she looks back on that year, and the next. She came out, saw me sitting there, head bowed over a book. She wanted to touch the nape of my neck. But didn't. She wasn't sure why. My neck was slender, white, like a child's, I often sat with my head over a book. I held the book over my knees, leaning forwards, my arms rested on my thighs. I read with my mouth open, stared into the air, moved my lips, noted something down on a slip of paper. She wanted to sit next to me and put her arm over my shoulder, but couldn't bring herself to do it. She passed me, running down the four steps, she stopped on the gravel and turned to me, not knowing what to say.

– Are you going for a run?

She nodded, she'd agreed to meet him, she felt she should tell me, but was unsure how her voice would sound if she said it. Then she found a way. She posed sweetly, thinking to please me. She cocked her head to one side, as lovers do without giving it a thought, and said:

– I've been invited.

– To do what?

– To go for a run.

– Who by? Him?

– Yes.

– Didn't you go running with him yesterday too?

– Yes, but I bumped into him by chance.

– And he's sent you a text?

– Yes.

She laughed, and then I laughed too. It was a bit of fun. It wasn't so dangerous after all. She wanted to give me a hug, but couldn't, not now. She stepped forward and stroked my cheek, and I said

– But isn't he married?

– Yes. But we're only going for a run, you know.

– But you think he's good-looking?

– He's athletic.

We looked at each other. It was a joke, a kind of game, she knew I'd bring it up again in the evening when we went to bed. She looked at me and said

– It's nothing to worry about.

– No, I think it's a good thing.

– What is?

– Your running with him. You can't *not* run with him just because he's a man, can you? We're not like that.

– No, we're not like that.

– Besides, I like thinking that you find him handsome.

– I didn't mean it that way.

– Didn't you?

– I don't know.

She had to tread carefully. And I said

– You seem to be blushing.

– Don't be daft.

I sat there smiling up at her, and she was unsure where she had me. Was it just a game, just something I came up with so we could fantasise about it when she got home? The sunlight was strong, she felt a rush of heat on her back and neck, and in her face too.

– I'm only blushing because of what you said.

– It suits you when you're embarrassed.

– Embarrassed?

– That's what it's called.

– I really must go.

— Yes, you must.

— I don't know how long I'll be.

— I'll be here.

— It's just that he wanted to show me a route that's possibly quite long.

— Be careful then.

— With what?

— When you run.

— I haven't got my phone. It's a hassle when you're running.

She felt free. That was something we gave each other, saying *yes* to whatever the other person wanted. It was in line with everything I said to her when we were naked together. That she could do whatever she wanted. She was a free spirit and must be true to that. Some day she might desire another man, and then she should do whatever she wanted with him, and come home to me afterwards and tell me about it. But she did *not*, she thought, want to do what she wanted, not everything. She didn't want to be unfaithful, for example. She wanted her life to remain exactly as it was. She must watch herself, she thought, and watch out for me too, so I wouldn't get upset, so that things wouldn't be spoiled between us.

No, she didn't think that. Not any more.

She had received the text early that morning. She'd guessed it might come, then she heard a muffled ping from her phone, it was an unknown number, and the moment she saw his name at the bottom of the text, she became suddenly aware of her body in the room, felt her own contours, her weight, her very existence, felt how the air touched her skin and the space it formed inside her as she took a breath in and slowly let it out again. It was a brief text, *Coming for a run?* he asked, adding that he wanted to go for a slightly longer run this time.

And she texted back: *Sure. Now?* And he replied, almost immediately: *Perfect.* She'd gone upstairs and changed, and then come out and talked with me, and now she was already on her way to meet him. She closed the gate behind her and started to run.

She was away for the whole day. When she came back she was filled with the experience, but she refused to let herself think about it. It had been pleasant, there was nothing dangerous about it, and now she'd come home to her normal life again. It was late in the afternoon, a family Saturday. I'd made pizza with the kids. We'd just finished eating when she came in. She told me all about where she'd been, and it came easily, she felt. She could give me a vivid description of the landscape and the distance she'd run. She went and took a shower, stood alone under the warm water. When she came out again, the kitchen was tidy, the kids had disappeared into their rooms, and I was out in the garden. She saw me through the window, walking back and forth, head bowed, she could hear I was cutting the grass.

She thought *what happens now?* then stopped thinking, she couldn't think, not about that. She went out into the garden, where I'd just finished the mowing. I stood there in an old T-shirt and cut-off jeans, my shoes stained with grass. I was still the man she knew so well, I walked towards her across the lawn with my shoulders hunched, and suddenly I seemed very small, frightened. But I didn't want her to see it, she realised. She saw it and was somehow touched. Touched as from a distance, as when watching a character who arouses pity in a series or movie. And even more powerful was the next thought that rose in her, the one she had avoided. He wanted something from her. It rose slowly in her body, like water, like black water in a house where everyone is asleep, she thought, brimming.

She put her hands on my shoulders. I looked at her, my face was blotchy, vulnerable and desperate. My bone structure was visible beneath my skin, the thin bridge of my nose stuck out like a beak between my cheekbones. I had hollows in my skull at the temples, which she had never noticed before. My eye sockets were deeper than she remembered. My blue, staring eyes seemed wider, they were bigger with each passing year. She took a deep breath and said

— Hello, my sweet, are you okay?

And that was all that was needed for it to pass, my colour returned and my fear seemed to melt away. I straightened up and acted casual. She leaned towards me, rested her head on my shoulder and felt my arms around her back. She kissed the bare skin on my upper arm and thought of him, of his skin, how it would feel against hers, under her hand, against her mouth.

A little later we sat at the table out in the garden, and she told me she'd been to a part of the forest she'd not known about. Ancient forestland, completely untouched. They'd run on soft springy moss, under pine trees that were hundreds of years old. She told me what they'd talked about, that he wanted her on a research project which his division were planning. She was flattered. But she didn't have the time, and wasn't even sure if her contract would permit it. Besides, she was concerned about taking on a project initiated by his division, there were regulations that made such cooperation difficult.

But he refused to give up, he'd talked very positively about her and wanted to help her progress. He was after something else too, she thought. Though she might be wrong, she wasn't sure, she wasn't accustomed to other men holding her gaze, not in the way he did. She liked it. She had held his gaze, she too, as though they were challenging each other. They'd looked into each other's eyes, a little too long. She told me all this, heard herself talking, heard her own voice as if she were speaking under running water. The rush of blood in her ears was like the roar of water, of the wind, or of a crowd in a distant room.

We sat in the garden until late. The crests of the trees grew dark around us, sucking in the darkness like cloth absorbing moisture. The sky was still light, turquoise, white, emerald and deep blue, ravaged by the setting sun. We sat in a clearing where everything above us was luminous, while the ragged summer shadows crept tight about our feet, beneath the table and in the grass. I lit some candles. My face flared up as I leaned across the table with the match in my hand.

She fetched her laptop and showed me a picture of him online. She could see I was a bit disappointed. Or at the very least, rather surprised. I said he looked like any other ordinary guy. He looked old, despite being younger than her. Like a middle-aged man from the 1960s, self-important, uptight and with neatly pressed trousers. And a terrible shirt. She listened as I went on, I was excited and happy, and failed to notice that she was feeling offended. But she was. She felt hurt on his behalf. We usually shared the same opinion about the people we met, but this was altogether different. She wanted to shut me up. She wanted to talk about him, to hear herself talk, to hear what she might say. She didn't know who he was until she talked about him to me, and she didn't want me to talk back.

But he wasn't the sort of man I'd pictured. I'd presumed that if she were to flirt with another man, he'd be fine-featured, less rugged and more androgynous. The kind of man I'd like too, a man I could have fallen for.

– He's a ski instructor.

– Yes, you told me.

– He's a dance teacher too, and a climbing instructor. He's a member of a gun club and wants to teach me how to shoot. In fact, he was a riding instructor too.

– And he wants to teach you to ride?

– Yes, and he goes running, as you know. He has the same interests as I do.

– Is he really a riding instructor?

– That was some years ago. But he still owns a horse.

She was proud of him, just like parents are proud of their children. No, like anyone who is in love and wants to tell everyone about the amazing qualities of this person who has stepped into their lives. She wanted to tell me about him. I was, after all, the person in whom she was used to confiding. And now she felt I was pursuing her. I wanted to see him as she saw him. I wanted to be her. I wanted to feel what she felt for him. And I said

– I don't really understand what you see in him.

– It's his body. I want to touch him.

– Where?

– In a dark room, perhaps?

I leaned forward; she felt my hand on her knee.

– Where on his body?

– His arms, his neck, I don't know, perhaps lower down on his stomach. He's quite athletic, you know. I feel like shoving my hand down his trousers, and touching the skin just above his groin. I have the urge to kiss him while I do it.

She spoke as though in her sleep, she went numb from hearing herself say these things.

– Do you find it difficult when I talk like this?

– Not at all. It's exciting.

– You really think so?

– Yes, it's exciting for me to listen to it. It turns me on.

– Of course, I don't *want* to do it, not for real. You do know that?

– But perhaps you'll do it anyway.

– I couldn't. I don't want to.

– Are you sure? Shouldn't we be able to make room for that, seeing as everything is so good between us?

There I sat. I was her husband. Several times a day I said that I loved her, but again and again I also said she had to be free, that her life was unfolding here and now, and she must live it freely. It was a summer's evening, soon night. Our life, all we shared, resembled no one else's, of that we were certain. And this was the only life for me. Big words, she thought, while at the same time basking in their warmth. She trusted the fact that I was always there, that my face always turned to her, glowing, like a deformed white flower. Our voices were audible to any passer-by, but no one could hear what we said. We looked just like any couple enjoying each other's company, talking intimately about things they can't discuss with anyone else. She straightened in her chair, and as if dragging it out of herself, she voiced the one thing that had troubled her all afternoon,

— I don't know if he likes me.

— I'm sure he does.

— I can't quite believe it.

— But it's obvious.

— How can you be so sure?

— You like him, and this sort of thing is almost always mutual. You've talked and exchanged emails. He invited you on a trip, you've gone running together twice. You say he looks into your eyes, and that you look into his. These are clear signs, you know that.

I felt safe again now, as I always did when she was at home, when we shared the same space. I leaned over to her, reassured her that it wasn't dangerous, that if she ever fancied someone else, for example this man, she should go with it, do something about it. It would, I said, suit us very well. I waved my arm out towards the garden, or beyond the garden, towards the neighbouring houses. I wanted so much to live another kind of life. I'd have done almost anything to escape being an ordinary man in a world that endlessly replicated itself, where everyone was identical to everyone else, and life seemed preordained. A kind of flat and narrow existence, I called it. I couldn't stand the thought of seeing myself or her like that. And she said she knew that. She liked it, even if she didn't quite understand it, or what it really implied.

I said – what did I say? – something about her having to follow everything that was most alive in her. Any ordinary man would have been jealous, would have made a scene, and been furious with this man who had quite shamelessly hit on another man's wife. But I was in a very good mood, it seemed, excited and eager to know what effect it had on her. Now that she was back at home, now that we were together, there were no limits to what could be. I said that the culture we lived in had always made such things possible for men. Wasn't it common for men to take mistresses, to have long-term extra-marital relationships? That was why Simone de Beauvoir hadn't wanted to get married, she was frightened of ending up with a man who lived as her father had lived, a wife and children in one house, a mistress in the other, going to and fro, between one life and the other. Male sexuality had been accommodated thus for centuries. But there was no reason to think sexuality was any less potent or different in a woman, so why shouldn't the situation be reversed? Think of Vanessa Bell, I said, think of Iris Murdoch, they both had relationships with other people, openly, to avoid hypocrisy and lies, and countless others had managed it too. But in our time, and here in Norway, any attempt at living in accordance to one's own vision had been swept away, all our acquaintances lived as though they were still in the 1950s, it was intolerable. Why shouldn't she do what so many men had done throughout history? I meant every word, she was certain. She remembered how frightened I'd looked when she came home, and then she forgot it. She thought that I was opening possibilities for her that she'd not seen before.

She said I was remarkable, and I said that I loved her. My face was radiant, almost manic, in the twilight. We got up to go in, we put our arms about each other and kissed, we giggled and felt each other under our clothes. Darkness grew out of the trees and air and grass and chairs. We stood for a long time holding each other, and then she freed herself, and we headed inside for bed.

She stood alone in the bathroom. She looked at herself in the mirror. She met her own gaze, held it, then could hold it no longer. She went to bed. She could hear me moving about, tidying and putting glasses in the dishwasher, opening and closing drawers. And then it went quiet. I was writing perhaps. She thought of the man who had placed his hand on the nape of her neck, and how she had stood quite still and let him do it.

She was almost asleep when I came to bed. She woke up again. She lay there and watched me pull my shirt over my head. I tossed it carelessly aside. My belt was undone already, I stepped straight out of my trousers, leaving them on the floor. I took off my underpants, stooping for a second and then straightening up. I was her husband, I stood naked before her, she wanted me to come and lie down.

We lay beside each other, and I whispered in her ear all the things I wanted her to do. She had always liked that, my words could almost make her come, but now she said

– Can't we just fuck?

and I said

– Right away?

and she said

– Yes, an ordinary Norwegian fuck,

and then we did it, or rather: I did it to her. She lay on her back, without moving, she parted her thighs, or I parted them for her, she can no longer remember, but I forced myself inside her. I lay *with* her, I lay *on* her, I laid her. I shoved my thing in her opening, shunted it in and out. A totally normal Norwegian fuck, fast, rhythmical, hard. She lay on her back, unable to keep her eyes open, unable to keep her mouth shut. She let herself be shoved up the bed. Let herself be laid, filled and taken, let herself be done to, and I was the one doing it. She saw my face over hers, sweating, hot, breathing with my mouth open, as if I were running.

She thought of the man she'd started to know. His neck, his arms, imagined him leaning over her. I leaned over her, took her without saying anything. It was good, even if it didn't last very long, and she liked it that way, fast, hard and without a word. She lay with her legs and arms sprawled to the side. She lay under a man who wanted her more than he wanted anyone or anything, she knew that, but was it enough? She didn't know, she didn't think about it, not now. I thrust myself into her hard, in and out, out and in, again and again and again and again. She forgot to think about him, and then she did not forget him again.

She had to say it, to shout it, to hear her own voice. She said *darling*. She said *darling, my darling*. She said *you're completely divine*. She said my name: *oh Jon, oh Jon, oh Jon, oh Jon*. She said *if we ever split up*. She said *though we'll never split up of course, but if*. And she said *then we'll have to have a secret affair, you and I, because I don't want to stop sleeping with you, you know that?* It was a sweet thing to say. And she saw the change that came over my face, that a light went on for me, or that a darkness fell, how else could she explain it? I was alone now, in this world that had been ours, hers and mine. She saw that I knew what had happened to her, I must know it now, she had finally said it. She called my name again, she thought about him and called for me. Her voice was tender and husky in that dark room, she felt it work its effect on me, that voice, a gentle moan. And it affected her too. We yelled, we both yelled loudly and for a long time, then it fell silent and it was over.

7

ONE EVENING LATER THAT AUTUMN TIMMY
came home; she'd been out riding, which made a strong
impression on our youngest boy. She was wearing riding
boots and tight jodhpurs. He'd never seen her in these
clothes before, and she told him she'd borrowed them.
She'd met a man who owned a horse and was going to
teach her to ride. She had borrowed them from him. An
acrid smell came from her, the boy came up in a rash and
his eyes itched. She hung the clothes in the hall, went for
a shower and came back looking more like herself again,
in her dressing gown and with wet hair.

But that night he woke up and remembered that his
mother now had a horse. He'd got it into his head that
this horse was very small. She couldn't live without this
horse. True enough, she had lived without it up until now
and been fine. But now that she knew of the horse's existence, how would things turn out? It was a brown horse, no
bigger than a dog that reached her knees. She left home
each evening to be with her horse. It visited her whenever
she was alone. It didn't like anyone else. It didn't like her
family. Or rather, it liked him and his brother, and perhaps
even their father too, but it was his mother it wanted to
be with. It waited for her at the end of our road, on the

edge of the forest. Sometimes it came and walked beside her without a word. Just her and the horse. Its mane was black, its pelt a rich brown, the colour of old logs, or new turned earth in a shaft of sunlight, like his mother's hair in the pictures he'd seen of her when she was a child long ago. Now she had black hair with a fringe, like the horse with its thick dark mane that hung over its eyes. They resembled each other, with large brown eyes and long dark eyelashes. Her horse stood and peered up at her. It contemplated her with a calm she'd never known before. To think such peace could exist. She saw herself in that big black unflinching horse-eye, she saw her life change there, and she said

– I want you in my life.

The horse continued to observe her, a dark, steady, insistent gaze. It was the horse that had said it. The horse wanted her in its life, and now she repeated its words. It leaned in to her, she felt the weight of that strong horse-body against her thigh. It pushed itself against her. And then it began to visit her at home. Each time she was alone in a room, the horse would come. It would stand by the wall, turn its head and watch her intently. Each time it would seem as though the horse had been waiting for her. She ought to have come sooner. It shook its mane, it shook its tail, and its coarse hair brushed against the wall and it crossed the floor towards her. Its hooves would clatter and scrape the hard parquet, leaving marks that everyone would see. Though that didn't bother her at all. She could think of nothing but the fact that she finally had a horse.

The horse wanted her on its back, wanted to take her with it. It grew, it was no longer a little horse that reached up to her knee, it was big. The horse grew so huge it filled the entire room. The boy's mother had to stretch up to put her arms around its neck. Now it was she who reached only to its thighs. In the beginning the horse had shrunk itself to fit into her life, but now it wanted to carry her away. And as soon as she let it have everything it asked for, it began to grow. It grew enormous, it filled her whole life, she could see nothing else.

He saw himself lying under the large belly of the horse. His mother was up on its back, he could see her riding boots, their soles, and he heard her voice, tender, intimate and filled with warm breath, so familiar to him. But she was talking to the horse, and as he listened to her voice, he heard that it was different, darker and deeper, and he couldn't understand what she said. He knew that when he woke up the next morning, the horse would have been to visit her again. And, true enough, he found its tracks on the floor, deep gashes in the parquet and stairs. It had scraped against the wall. It had gnawed the chairs. It had gnawed the edge of our bed. It had been in the bathroom, he could see it had peed on the floor in the corner, leaving a large pool of golden acrid urine. It had been thirsty, and in its search for water it had gnawed at the edge of the bath. It had bitten off a gigantic piece. The porcelain bore the marks of huge teeth, he found the piece on the floor and placed it carefully back so no one would see what the horse had done. He stood watching as the porcelain grew together, and the cracks smoothed away. On its way out of the house, the horse had chewed up his father's shoes that stood in the hallway, and he heard me say:

– What's *happening* here?

But the horse wasn't bothered. Nor was the boy's mother, she thought only about her fine horse. She took the horse into work, it stood under her desk, she put her hand between her knees and found its warm head there. She caressed its pointy, buckled, glossy and mobile ears. She placed two fingers on its cold wet muzzle. She guided her hand into its mouth and felt its long yellow teeth. She let it bite her. She sat very still and let the horse do what it wanted to her. When she got home in the early evening, she brought her hand to her face and sniffed it. She was happy to have found this horse, happy that such a fine horse existed in the world and that it was hers. And he, our little son, was happy too. He hoped that she would tell me about the horse soon, since he was sure I didn't yet know she had it. She would allow me to sniff her hand and then say *Can you tell what I smell of now?* And I would answer that she smelled of horse. I would say *How lucky you are to have such a fine horse, I am so happy for you.*

He imagined a brown horse with a coarse black mane, at first it was very small and then it grew very big. He was the youngest in the house, and he liked animals more than anything else. He inhabited these rooms together with us, sat at the table, lay in his narrow bed, ran across the parquet floors. He kept close to us, always, as often as he could, and our voices went right into his body.

8

ON NEW YEAR'S EVE SHE GOT UP LONG BEFORE anyone else in the house. She managed to stick to her plan, and was out on her skis by seven in the morning. It was still so dark she had to wear a headlamp. She had bought a new one for me for Christmas, a rather expensive, light-weight one with a rechargeable battery, which she now borrowed. Plump snowy troll-like shapes loomed at the edges of her vision. She was scared she might encounter an elk, fresh tracks zigzagged across the path, and she noticed a deep hollow in the snow where a large animal must have gone onto its side, lost its balance. Could an elk lose its balance in this deep fluffy snow? It seemed even less likely that an animal would have lain down to rest. She stopped for a moment and breathed, the ski tracks were pristine, the snowplough must have been here recently. Or more correctly, the *grooming machine*, one of those terms Timmy used so casually. Whatever its name, it hadn't been long since it had passed by. It was clear that between the snowplough and her arrival, only one skier had been here, but his tracks – and she was certain it was a man – came to an abrupt end. His tracks simply vanished at the top of a hill, as though he'd been lifted up into the sky. She was a little frightened of the dark, more than a little, and tried not to think too much about the possibility of meeting an elk. She continued up the slope, concentrating her mind on her technique, pushing herself just hard enough to feel her body respond to the effort. She felt strong. She was now one of those people who could cover vast distances, and she'd gone further than she intended before deciding to turn back. She headed swiftly down again, it was light now and many other skiers were out, mainly middle-aged men skiing alone, all with self-consciously straight backs and a determined, elegant kicking action, particularly, she noticed, when they met her. Occasionally she'd overtake one with a feeling of a triumph.

She saw nobody she knew, and had decided not to look for anyone either. She hadn't even taken her phone with her. She didn't need to meet Gunnar every time she went out, she needed nothing more than this, to get out early before anyone else, and to go fast on her skis. She turned off the headlamp, but left it to dangle round her neck, where anybody who wanted could see it. Perhaps they'd think she'd been out skiing all night. Two elderly women appeared ahead, skiing slowly side by side, she had to go to the very edge of the track to avoid bumping into them. She used her poles frequently, moving fast and enjoying her mastery over speed. Life was simple, right now it had never been difficult, she had mastery over her body and technique, her equipment was good and she handled herself well. She had mastery over existence itself, she was the person she wanted to be.

She was back home before nine, stamped off the snow on the steps and carried her skis into the hallway. She unlaced her boots and kicked them off, and went into the kitchen where I'd lit a fire in the new clean-burning wood stove. We'd stopped using electricity for heating and switched to wood burning, it was more economical, greener, created an ambiance and gave that *vintage* touch, as she said, poking fun at the middle-class values we'd made our own. We were mildly socially aware and quite sporty, although nobody used these words now, we said we liked to stay informed, that we were active, and liked to keep on the go. She pulled off her outdoor clothes and hung them over a chair to dry. The room was light, warm and tidy, the newspapers lay unopened on the table. I'd taken them in, she saw that I'd cleared the snow and made a neat path to our postbox. The kids were still asleep, or at least in bed, she could feel that sleep reigned over the house, even the furniture was at rest, the chairs standing with open laps. I was probably in my study down in the basement. No doubt I'd heard her come in. She let the tap run until the water was ice cold and filled a glass. (Blue glass, hand-blown, bought on holiday in Italy.) She drained it in one big gulp, as always. Cold water in her mouth, down through her throat and chest, settling in her stomach. She refilled it again and drank the second glass as she considered what needed doing. Almost nothing, she'd already prepared the turkey yesterday evening, she wanted to make a salad, otherwise everything would look after itself. But first she wanted a cup of coffee and to read the papers, to sit at the table and luxuriate in the feeling of having done a good workout. She started the coffee machine and stretched while she waited. She nibbled the head off a marzipan Christmas pig, it belonged to one of the kids — they weren't really keen on marzipan anyway. She thought that she should take up yoga again. She took her cup — white porcelain, plain — to the table where she sat and browsed through the newspapers. There wasn't much to read, or perhaps she couldn't concentrate on what there was. She was eager to tell me about how far she'd been, and about the elk tracks. She opened her laptop and looked at the news. A fire, a bus accident, something about the weather, a piece about the year's craziest excuses. She didn't open her email, or check her phone. She rested in the tranquillity of the familiar. She heard a door and assumed it was one of the kids going to the loo, but then moments later she heard footsteps on the stairs above, it was me coming down. She straightened up a little and pulled her laptop towards herself, allowing me to see her, before she lifted her head to say hello.

She was still fresh and red-cheeked, she could feel it herself, she'd been out and was pleased with herself. She gave a little stretch as I crossed the room towards her, then she felt my hands on her shoulders, her neck, down her back. I closed my hands over her breasts. They drifted down towards her waist, I felt her skin under her vest, cool to the touch, I grabbed her hips, she knew I liked that, it hinted at sex, which was probably why I did it; it was a signal. I leaned over her and kissed her on the neck, her cheek, her neck again and then the nape of her neck. She turned to face me, and we kissed each other on the mouth. Our lips were dry, so we opened our mouths and kissed with tongues, let our lips grow wet and hot. Everything swelled and yearned to be touched. She reckoned we had just enough time to go to bed before the kids got up. I still had my pyjamas on, she stroked my inner thigh. She could feel I'd had the same thought. She put her hand on my crotch, outside my pyjama bottoms. She told me how much good it had done her to go skiing, that she'd seen nobody out before daylight. She told me about the elk tracks, about the hollow where an animal had lain, and about the tracks of the skier who had vanished into thin air. She described the other skiers, those who'd arrived only as it grew light, and how they'd mainly been men.

— Typical. All the women are at home making the dinner.

— Precisely. I'm so lucky not to have to live like that.

— You think you're lucky?

She stroked the small of my back and said

— Yes, very lucky,

and I said *you are indeed*; there was a pause, then she laughed with a look of feigned outrage, and I said that I'd meant to say *I* was lucky too. We both laughed, and she said

— Have you had a good morning?

She wanted to ask whether I'd done any writing, but stopped herself. She knew I didn't like her to ask whether I'd been reading or writing, or what I'd been doing. It was best not to enquire in case I hadn't achieved anything. She'd learned that I didn't like to talk about what I was doing, my determination flagged every other day, every other hour, and then I didn't want to discuss my children's books or my popular science articles. She also knew that I would sometimes want to after all, that I'd suddenly be eager to talk about my writing, she just never knew when. Which was why she just asked if I'd had a good morning, and I said

— I've been reading Simone de Beauvoir. I don't know why I haven't read her before.

— Surely you've read her before?

— Well, yes, but I put it aside, and I shouldn't have. She writes with such vitality, such freedom, she writes about love, about devotion, she talks completely openly, it seems. Although it's quite obvious she's talking to Sartre, that her focus is on him and her relationship with him. She writes to him from the US, she went there to visit Nelson Algren, she had a relationship with him, you must know.

— I don't remember who Nelson Algren was.

— He was an author. I wouldn't say things were exactly easy between them, although suddenly any problems seem to vanish, when she mentions how they had slept together early one morning. In Chicago, I think, in the cabin they stayed in perhaps. Can you imagine? She writes about sleeping with another man who she's involved with, telling Sartre how this relationship with Algren has suddenly grown so tender and close, after she'd thought it was so impossible.

— And that was how they lived?

— Yes, but in other letters I've read between the two of them, jealousy is clearly at work. They weren't meant to feel jealousy, but it seems they did. When one of them falls in love with someone else, the other has to find someone to fall in love with too. As though they're trying to outdo each other. But not this time. She gets so deeply attached to Algren, I think, and she's full of it when she writes to Sartre, and then it seems so simple. As if it were inescapable, and thus absolutely fine.

– How did he respond?

– Who?

– Sartre?

– I don't know. I don't have his letters from that period.

– Shall we have a little lie-down?

– It's already gone nine, we'll have to be quick.

– Do you think they're awake?

– I don't know.

We followed each other into the bedroom and closed the door as quietly as we could. We had quite big children now, we'd grown up together. We couldn't count how many times we'd slept together, not that it was important, we weren't planning to stop. It was more fun to count the times we'd slept with other people before we'd met. Once we'd been inexperienced and awkward in our different worlds. Once we'd hidden from our parents to take off our clothes with boyfriends and girlfriends, and now here we were hiding from our children to be naked together. She pulled off her top and leggings while I watched, then lay down and waited for me to take off her pants (she didn't like the word knickers, so I never used it). She was wearing boxers anyway. I pulled them off with studied slowness, and said

– You're beautiful, and look, your pants have left an imprint on your skin.

I ran the tips of my fingers lightly over her skin and showed her. Her pale skin, delicate and winter-white, and chilly from being outside. She knew I liked the fact she was pale in the winter, I used to say that it made her body clearer somehow, and now she had a distinct flame-coloured pattern from the elastic round her hips and deep marks from the seams around her thighs.

– They're a bit tight, these pants.

– But it's beautiful. It's like nude clothing.

– Nude clothing!

– You could go around like that all the time.

– You'd like that. Everyone seeing me.

– Yes, I would.

– But only you think I'm that beautiful.

– Not at all. You just wait and see.

– Wait and see what?

Intimate chatter. Meaningless, childish, flirtatious exchanges between two people who know each other well. Or, at least, we had reason to believe we knew each other, we lived in the belief that we knew each other better than anyone else ever could, we'd built our own shadow republic of adult love on that conviction, and on hints and stolen glances over the children's heads. Everything we said to each other now, we had said many times before, the words needed only to match the actions of our hands. She pulled off my T-shirt, ran her hands over my back, pulled me down to her. She heard me say something, something about her, about her hands, or about her hips, or the way she held me. She put her hand down my pyjamas and touched me, closed her hand around my penis, and pulled the foreskin back. It felt like delicate fabric, wrinkled, taut, wrinkled, taut, a thinly worn fabric that had grown soft and smooth from being used so much, easily torn beneath her fingertips. I lay on top of her, supporting myself with straight arms, I placed my face over hers and looked into her eyes making her look into mine – that was something I did with all of them, made them look into my eyes, I needed it, just like I always had to sleep with everyone, she thought to herself. She liked thinking things I didn't know she was thinking. She opened herself with two fingers, and guided my penis towards the opening, the lips were moist here, but not so wet further in, a slight tug and she felt me pull out and then enter again. I did this many times, slowly, testing, exploring, with great seriousness. The inner lips were resistant, but then it grew more slippery and she felt herself open up. But I was too quick now, and it hurt, me too probably, she noticed, or perhaps she didn't, but realised it when I pulled out again. I moved further out, making short movements, it helped, and suddenly we were there, in that moment of surrender, of embrace, of belonging one with the other. We held our fear and boredom at bay, she lifted her hips, she wanted me all the way in, deep inside, she liked that thought, it was a fundamental principle, one might say: *to go deep inside*. And it wasn't painful, not for her and clearly not for me. She stopped talking, allowing her voice to be forced from her mouth with her breath each time I thrust myself into her, she pronounced an open, extended *ah* followed by more air, over and over again, the same sound – *ah! ah! ah! ah!* – and that did something to me, she knew it, and it did something to her too. We made noises of pleasure and

99

desire and greed, but then she suddenly remembered the kids. She looked up at me, now she was the one panicking, and it was me who said

— They can't hear us. The door is closed.

— Perhaps we should lock it.

— Maybe, but I'm not coming out of you now, I don't want to come out of you, not ever, which means we'll have to cross the floor together.

And so she closed her eyes, or grew unaware of what she did, stopped thinking, lost sight of herself, she let herself fall downwards again as I moved on her, towards her, in her. She put her hands on my back, and felt me shove her further up the bed. I supported myself on one hand and held her hips with the other, she liked that, we must both have liked it, I often used to hold her like that, around her pelvis. She started making noises again, and then she heard the door handle go, it was resolutely shoved down, I heard it too and let myself roll off beside her, reluctantly, my mouth gaping so comically that she burst out laughing. Our youngest son was standing in the doorway. He said

— Aren't you two up yet?

and I lay there pretending to be half asleep, my arms covering my face, and said

— Are you already awake? We'll get up soon. How about you go and watch telly?

and luckily he wanted to. He left the door open, but we'd done this many times before, we could do it quietly, slowly, without the kids hearing, even when they were in the next room. She turned onto her side, shoved her bum towards me, and pulled the pillow to her, she liked to hold it in front of her face. She let herself be taken, she thought – no, she had no thoughts – but that was what she wanted, to be taken, to be done to, and she wanted to scream, but couldn't, not even into the pillow. Giving voice to our desire, generally intensified that desire, but being *unable* to make any noise, intensified it too, oddly enough. She breathed fast into the pillow, smelling the scent of bedlinen that had been dried outside, bedlinen that grew damp with her breath, warm and heavy, like when we kissed for a long time and she inhaled the warm used air from my mouth.

And then our youngest son called to me, his voice clear and open. He felt secure in his existence and secure in us, he knew we were there for him, he shouted

– Daddy, can you help me put the telly on?

And she realised I was incapable of answering, and shouted, rather too loud:

– Daddy will come soon!

And it was true, we both saw the joke, but we didn't laugh, not immediately, she just snorted and I gave an offended grunt. I tried not to lose focus, but it was impossible, not a chance. We heard him getting closer, he was on his way back, he wanted to be sure I hadn't forgotten my promise to help him, he wanted to be close to us, to his mummy and daddy. He sought warmth, needed our voices, our bodies, needed to know that we knew he was there, that we were watching over him, and he said

– What are you two laughing at?

He wanted to join in, to laugh with us, and was about to get up into the bed, but I threw myself out, saying I'd come with him; my pyjama bottoms were round my knees and now I pulled them up, bending over in an attempt to stop anything from showing under the fabric; it was easy to see though, so I pressed my lower arm against my crotch and said

– I'll come now and help you put the TV on.

And heading out of the room, I turned to her, we smiled at each other, we were out of breath, flushed and frustrated. She was still lying in the bed and shoved her hand under the duvet, she made sure I saw her shove her hand under the duvet, we might still be in with a chance, and she shouted

– I'll have a shower, will you come too?

and I said yes, conspiratorially, my voice laden with excitement, I could never resist her crazy ideas, and I closed the door softly behind me. She knew why I'd closed it, and she tried for a bit, but it wasn't happening, not now.

No matter, a sweet bliss ran warm and alive inside her, she felt protected by it, it lifted her, just as getting up early to go for a ski could lift her for hours, just as reading the papers and having a coffee afterwards, just as yoga, or push-ups and sit-ups, or holding the plank position for a minute or two lifted her and made life translucent, helped her to cope. She'd get a bit down, find something to bring her up again, feel good, more than good, and then get a bit down again. She could dip beneath the surface at any time, but she was good at giving herself what she needed to come up again, she was, and she knew it. And now she got out of bed and went for a shower.

She'd managed to wash her hair before I came in and she locked the door behind me. I took off my pyjama bottoms and joined her in the shower. We put our arms around each other and kissed under the running water. Her hand went around my penis, it was softer, smaller, but began to grow, and then she turned her back to me, and leaned against the wall with her hands spread flat, and her cheek equally flat against the tiles, as though someone had pushed her hard against the wall. She moved her bottom towards me and spread her legs, felt me fumble and miss, before I entered her, with my fingers first and then with my penis. I pushed myself up inside her, she noticed that the water was streaming in my face and turned the shower head to the wall. I wasn't quite hard yet, she felt it, and I began to talk, so it would get bigger faster, so I'd come quicker, before anyone could interrupt us again. I asked if she had touched herself, and who she had thought about while she did it, and she replied *Wouldn't you like to know!* It worked, she felt me, long and hard, forcing my way in, and she grew wetter, and she felt that too, and I said

— Imagine if you had a visitor today. Imagine if he came and got into bed with you, while I was in the kitchen looking after the kids.

— Then I'd have been lying in there underneath another man. Just imagine.

And she heard me make a noise, a deep moan, as she let herself be pushed against the wall, but she heard something else too, a ring at the door, unbelievable, someone was actually ringing at the door, this early, on New Year's Eve, and moments later we heard voices in the hallway.

Our youngest son came and tried the bathroom door, Una Birgitte was here, he said. Una Birgitte was our neighbour. Timmy looked at me and shook her head, it was hopeless, and we heard our pale, little, wide-eyed boy say

— Why have you locked the door?

and she felt it slide out of her with a resigned squelch, wet and limp, *such a poor disappointed willy*, she wanted to say, but it wouldn't have been funny right now, so she decided to save it. Instead she put her hand on my face and stroked my cheek, and said *you stay here*, and said *we'll think of something, we'll put a film on for them and come back to bed a bit later*. She touched my penis lightly, as if to hint that I could do something myself in the meantime, it reacted under her fingers, she felt it, then she dried herself with a towel, quickly and ineffectually, pulled on her dressing gown and went out to talk to Una Birgitte, who had come to borrow something or invite us over for coffee.

My daughter was meant to have been there too, she'd spent Christmas with her mother, so she should have been with us for New Year, but she wanted to go to a party instead. I missed my daughter, I always did. But we'd talked it over and agreed it was a good thing, it was better for her to be out enjoying herself with kids her own age rather than being stuck here with us. Timmy habitually said things like that to me, pointing out the upside of things. I'd needed that badly when we first got together. Not only had I separated from another woman to be with her, but I'd separated myself from my daughter too.

When Una Birgitte was gone, Timmy found me in our eldest son's room. He was showing me a game, rather unwillingly, since he'd have preferred to play in peace. It was typical of me to seek out one of the kids when someone came to visit. Especially when I was so keen for them all to be at home. I was still in my pyjamas and T-shirt, I was the man she knew better than anyone else. That was how she thought of me. And it felt so comfortable to slip back into the safety of our shared world now. She whistled at me and watched my face light up and, smooth out, like a soft fabric. It was so easy for her to make me happy. So simple. And she liked to observe it.

– How about you come with me instead? she said.

I got up and followed her. She put her hand on my face, felt my hand reach down to the small of her back, pulled away for an instant as I went to kiss her, just to observe again how easy it was to make me feel safe, simple, manly and contented.

She had always said, when she was working as a GP, that it was part of the job to reformulate experiences so they were easier to bear. Patients often needed to recalibrate their understanding of themselves, to learn, for example, to live with chronic diseases. And she applied this technique to herself too, it was her way of staying afloat, almost everything could be reformulated so as to seem positive. And now it was so long since she'd gone out for her morning ski that she needed to lie naked in bed with me, we both needed it. I put on a movie that both our sons wanted to see, Wes Anderson's *Fantastic Mr. Fox*, I wanted to see it myself too, I said, but my desire to go to bed with her was greater. So when the film had started, we went into the bedroom and she locked the door as gently as she could.

We got undressed quickly, side by side, like children going for a swim, and slipped under the duvet, not like children, but as adult lovers who knew what they were about. Hands went where they were wanted, where they had been before. She stretched out on her back, I lay at her side, she lifted her thigh across me so I could enter her while she touched herself. She used one hand to hold her top lips open, tight and smooth, with the other she manipulated herself with two fingers. I pushed my penis into her slowly, it struck a point she knew well, a point that released such intense sensations that she'd been known to come just from that, without touching herself at all. She swelled around me, flesh thickened between us, we merged, we no longer knew who was who or what was what, except that it was she who lay with her eyes closed and without moving, while I moved over her and spoke softly and lovingly into her ear.

I said she had been visited by a man she desired, and that she had locked herself with him in the bedroom while I had to take care of the kids so they wouldn't notice. I described him to her, tall, slender, light in his movements, told her what he wanted to do with her. I went back and forth between the kids and the locked door. I stood outside listening to the noises she made. She liked it when I said that, her head went from side to side on the pillow, and I liked it too, but it wasn't enough, not for me. I said that I would prefer to be in there with her, watching her being taken by him, I wanted to see his cock, a word I used when I was with her, said that I wanted to see it grow long and hard, and get wet from being inside her, I wanted to see him thrust himself in and out of her. She did not open her eyes as I said this, but she knew I was looking at my own penis, imagining that it belonged to another man, as I slid in and out of her. She made a noise, no, she didn't make it, it came of itself, a gentle howl. Her thighs shook, she felt it. A delicious sensation. I asked if I could watch just once, watch her doing it with someone else. She was being shoved up the bed because I was thrusting harder, she opened her eyes and discovered my face closer to her own than she'd expected, I was watching her, eager to see the pleasure flicker on her lips, over her eyelids, the way she tossed her head as though there was something wrong, but of course there wasn't, and she said *yes, yes you can*, and a moment later she cried *yes, yes, yes*, and then she grabbed the pillow, put it over her face, yelled into it. Soon after, she felt me come too, quietly, with a sort of stifled groan, nothing more, and suddenly we both lay there motionless, silent, listening out to see if the kids had heard us. But they hadn't, we were quite certain, both of us.

We got up, got dressed and made lunch together. The film was almost finished, the end of *Fantastic Mr. Fox* is a let-down in contrast to its promising beginning, but our sons sat huddled together with their mouths open, seemingly oblivious to the fact we'd even left the room. She had put the turkey in the oven ages ago, it needed to stay in for three hours and would be ready soon. Now she made the sauce, while I boiled the potatoes and sprouts and laid the table, and I grumbled that she'd taken most of the responsibility for lunch, it was so typical, I felt like a typical man with a typical woman, and that wasn't how I wanted it to be, everything closed in around me, I said, everything was so limited and ordinary, and then she said

— You're forgetting something.

— What?

— You're forgetting that you make the food almost every day.

And then I was happy again, as she'd anticipated, and she told me that Una Birgitte had invited us over to their place later. But that didn't make me happy, and I said

— What, tonight, on New Year's Eve?

— Yes, but we're just here at home on our own. And so are they. They thought the kids could sit downstairs in the basement and watch a film together, and they've got some wine and cheese for us. I thought it might be quite nice. It's easy and spontaneous, nothing formal, don't you think?

The minute she'd accepted Una Brigitte's invitation, she realised I wouldn't approve, and that she should have consulted me first. But she hadn't wanted to say no. She couldn't see any reason to refuse; besides, it suited her well enough. She liked things to be happening. The effects of her morning ski had already worn off, she wasn't feeling as harmonious any more. And as Una Birgitte sat in our kitchen drinking coffee, we still hadn't managed to get our act together in bed. Now, post-orgasm, she'd have been happy to sit quietly for an hour or two. But she knew she'd soon be on the lookout for something else to do. Then it would be nice to be with Una Birgitte and Paul Edvin drinking wine and talking. She liked talking to people, she could get away from herself. Which was similar to the reason I gave for *not* liking social occasions, I lost myself. I'd always been a bit cranky in her opinion, but during those first years she hadn't minded it. She'd taken a lesson from it, no longer saying *yes* to absolutely everything that came along, and becoming more aware of her own needs. But lately more and more things seemed to be an issue for me. Besides which, she'd stopped saying *yes* to all my suggestions too. She knew I'd prefer to be alone with the kids, and with her, but she'd accepted the invitation instantly without talking to me.

And now it was five o'clock, and we sat at dinner, like so many other families in the country, and she saw I'd already begun to dread it. She'd made a stuffing with mushrooms and onions and garlic and basil and salt, stirred into sour cream. The turkey had been in the oven for three and a half hours, I'd boiled the potatoes and made a gravy from the giblets. She'd found the recipe for the salad the day before, with blue cheese and red onions. It was rather too strong with such rich food, and the kids didn't eat it, but she carved the perfect pale slices of turkey and served. It was essential to us that she carve. We'd have looked like a family in the 1950s if I'd done it, we said, when our eldest boy asked why we always did it that way. She felt light, triumphant. The turkey wasn't too dry, it was lean and white, though a bit difficult to slice, or perhaps the knife needed sharpening, she was annoyed with herself for not having done it. She raised her glass to me, and then the children. She stretched her foot out and stroked my shin, expecting me to smile, but *no*. We'd had a good time together (after a few false starts) yet its effect on me was already wearing off, clearly. She went to get the hot gravy from the cooker, and on her return she walked behind me. She placed the gravy boat in front of me, then leaned over me and ran her fingers through my hair. I looked up at her. My eyes were glazed, my lips pursed, she hoped I wasn't about to start to cry.

– Are you upset?

– Not at all.

But I must have been upset, or irritated, verging on tears of frustration. I never wanted to admit I was cross, it was too petty, cross should have been eradicated from the register of human emotion, I'd once said. But she knew from experience that I could feel very put out, agitated to the point of having to go and lie down. This was clearly going to get awkward if she couldn't turn it around. She slid her hand down the front of my shirt, rubbed my chest around my heart area. She felt it beating hard and fast, then she bent down and whispered in my ear:

– You made me come so wonderfully.

I looked up at her; with her fingers in my hair, she drew my face towards hers and kissed me. I was usually the first to open my lips, this time she did, pushing her tongue against mine, giving me a long kiss. A few smacking noises ensued, causing our oldest boy to groan in despair, he was painfully embarrassed, but she placed her hand in front of my face as if to shield me, and said:

– Shh. I'm just kissing your dad a bit.

He produced another noise, a sort of growl. It was almost comical, but it wasn't meant to be amusing, he was expressing his disgust, he couldn't bear to look at us. She didn't remove her hand but kissed me again in the little space her hand created around my face. She bit my bottom lip and looked into my eyes.

– We'll only stay until after the fireworks, and then we'll come home and go to bed, all right?

– I don't want to do the fireworks with Paul Edvin. Are he and I supposed to do the fireworks while you and Una Birgitte serve cakes, is that it?

I was getting worked up, she could see that. Paul Edvin was a sore point with me. He was a teacher, he taught Norwegian and had more than an average interest in literature, music and film. Besides which, he liked to stay at home when he wasn't at work – social events made him as shy and uncomfortable as they did me – so when we first got to know them, I'd thought he could be the friend I'd never had. But something went wrong, we didn't find any common ground, our conversations never got beyond the politely conventional. Timmy said that even such exchanges had some value, but I felt deeply frustrated over the fact I could never discuss anything spontaneously with him. And since Una Birgitte believed blind in gender segregation, she always lowered her voice and talked to Timmy when she had anything real to say. Thus excluded, Paul Edvin and I were left to cultivate that male form of human interaction which involved giving each other brief lectures on one thing or another. I could never be myself, the person I wanted to be, something I'd find untenable, and which would eventually drive me to take my leave and march off home.

Timmy stroked the short, clipped hair on the back of my neck, it felt smooth like fur, like sleek water-resistant otter fur; she was usually the one to cut it. She walked over to the kitchen worktop and picked up her phone. She'd left it on the windowsill face down, and she'd put it on to silent so she wouldn't be waiting for it to ring. She'd let half the day pass before checking it, so as to be sure of finding a nice message on it. He'd presumably sent several already. She'd even started to think she might prefer not to receive any texts from Gunnar right now, a part of her wanted to be left in peace, with me and the kids. Anyway, she thought, whatever this was between them, it would almost certainly pass. But now she was overwhelmed by an intense, agonising longing. It occurred to her that he'd had similar thoughts, deciding to find tranquillity in the ordinary, the lawful and safe, in his marriage and family. That must be why he hadn't texted her, and suddenly it seemed so unfair, so wrong, almost bad form. She typed a short text – opening with a bright *Hi there!* – then changed it to something more downbeat. She said she'd been out skiing, and that she'd looked for him. She put down her phone and returned to the table. As she walked past me, she put her hand on my neck, giving it a squeeze with her fingers, saying she'd got a text from her sister. Then, without waiting for a response, she said

– I'll do the fireworks with Paul Edvin. You can just go home when you're fed up. It's pretty likely that at least one of your sons will want to go home too.

This inspired the exact level of happiness in me she'd predicted. I nodded in the direction of our youngest boy, who we'd always agreed resembled me most, and said

– I think you might just be right.

He was sitting staring into thin air. He was thinking about something, chewing on his turkey and potatoes with an open mouth and drinking orangeade, depositing greasy smudges on his glass from his mouth and fingers. He had spilled gravy down his white shirt, an oblong stripe that grew wider at the bottom like a map of Norway.

She reached her foot out towards me under the table, touched my knee with her toes. I looked across at her, my face softened, I raised my glass to her. She'd made it easier for me, and so it was easier for her too, it would be all right.

9

ONE THURSDAY IN FEBRUARY SHE CAME HOME
late. She'd been out skiing with him, and they'd gone a
long way. Each time they went further than they'd intended. It became impossible to turn back. They wanted
to show each other how strong they were, how far they
could go. They wanted to show each other how different
everything was, how vital and dynamic, when they were
together. Besides, it had been such a perfect day out there.
A gentle February breeze in the trees, and wet snow in
the morning which turned crisp and hard as evening approached. The darkness closed about them, there were no
other skiers out, just the two of them. The moon, one-
eyed and monochrome, shone down on them, turning the
snow and slender spruce trees blue, in perfect stillness.

She heard the sound of their skis and poles in the
frozen snow. They stopped and looked around, talked for
a moment. Their voices seemed muffled and intimate out
here, padded somehow, she heard herself as though from
inside the snow. It would soon be night, and they decided
they must turn back. She was hot and aching, and the way
back was longer than she remembered. She went ahead of
him on the downhill slopes, aware of him watching her.
He evaluated everything she did, she felt his gaze follow
her rhythm. She dug her poles in on the gentler slopes,

forceful and energetic, rising onto the balls of the feet and pushing herself forward, crouching low to minimise wind-drag on every little hill. She enjoyed the speed, and she enjoyed being watched by him.

And just once she fell; leaning too far forward at a corner she plunged sideways into a snowdrift. It was soft and deep, she didn't hurt herself, she just got a shower of powdery snow on her face and neck. She felt like a child. Might it have been like that, that the happiness rose inside her like a child? Yes, that was it exactly: she lay deep in snow unable to get up. He came after her and swerved to a halt beside her, neatly and confidently, and held out his hand to help her. His smile in that moment would fix itself in her mind, first as an image she could conjure up when she was in bed at night, or when she was at work. Then later as an image that would hound her day after day, like a disturbing sound, but she still didn't know that. He pulled her up and asked if she was all right. But he didn't let her go, they stood holding hands. Then finally letting go he helped her brush off the snow. He had removed his ski gloves, his hands were big and warm. Their faces drifted towards each other, then away again, like two luminous planets that seem to gravitate towards each other in an otherwise impenetrable dark. They smiled, and started talking about skiing techniques. Though, surely they can't have done? Well, in fact they could have talked about anything, the meaning of what they said lay not in the words, but in how they were said.

But she had to get home now. As did he. She had said she'd be back before it got late, whatever that meant, before bedtime at least. He took the lead on the final path down towards the car park. He put her skis next to his. She watched as he stretched up to the ski box on the roof of the car, the movement ran through his body, definite and gentle. They'd taken his car, as usual, and now she was sitting in the passenger seat, being driven home by him. She sent me a text message, received no reply. Not a good sign. She hoped I'd gone to bed, but doubted it. I was probably waiting, going from room to room, irritated or anxious again.

She knew that. I was always agitated when she got back later than she said. It had happened once, and she'd prom-ised it would never happen again, but it did, once, twice, then frequently. The first time she was late home we were meant to go for a dirty weekend. Not a phrase either of us liked, nonetheless we'd started to use it. We were just going to the cottage together. The kids would stay with her parents, and we'd drive from home straight after work on Friday. She'd arranged to go to the climbing centre with him after lunch, her work gave her two hours off a week for sports activities, and he'd said he wanted to give her a climbing lesson. He did, and they lost track of time. She hung there eight metres up on the wall, and he stood beneath her holding the rope and the belay device. He secured her, as they say; she liked to think about what that meant. He shouted up at her, telling her where she could find a grip, *out a little to the left, slightly higher, can you feel it?* Whenever she reached a difficult bit, he'd tell her she was doing well, that she was great. Her legs were strong and she felt that helped her, he told her so. Afterwards he drove her home. She'd got a text from me asking *should I worry something's happened to you or have you just started to get flippant about us?* But she had not, she didn't feel the least bit flippant, not about me, nor us, nor anything else, she said later that night when we'd finally arrived at the cottage and made dinner together, still quarrelling. I'd stood and looked at her, and said *I'm glad about that, at least.*

And then they'd gone climbing and forgotten to look at the clock again, they'd gone running, several times, and each time they ran further than planned and came back late. Then the ski season started, and he invited her to go on a day trip. He'd taken time off work that day and asked if she wanted to join him, it would be like having a meeting, he'd said. He said it with the same kind of laughter in his voice that she had started to imitate, a merciless laugh, metallic and bright, that practically glinted, like a trumpet blasting in your sleep. He laughed at everything, nothing was too dangerous, it helped her that she'd begun to resemble him. What they were doing presented no danger to anyone at all. It was simple, they liked each other, they had shared interests, they had become good friends. That was why their trips went on longer than they'd intended.

She announced that she didn't like having fixed times at which to get home when she went out. She heard me repeat the words, *fixed times*, in disbelief. I asked if she'd become a teenager again, if I was a daddy to her or if we were still husband and wife. Increasingly often she heard me talk like that, in dramatic and drastic terms. I worked myself up, my eyes filled my face, she could see their whites, my hands shook with rage, I threw a half-opened milk carton. She had to help me wipe the floor afterwards, it didn't seem right to sit and watch. She couldn't see why I was reacting like this. She didn't understand why I would ask if we were still husband and wife.

I was talking, she said, as though she'd been unfaithful, which she certainly hadn't been. She heard me scoff at the word – *unfaithful* or *not unfaithful* – it was beneath our dignity to use such a word. I said that she could go ahead and sleep with him or with anyone else, so long as she didn't start getting flippant about us. I wasn't going to stop using that word now that I'd found it. I felt I'd been treated flippantly, just tossed aside, she heard me say. It summed up everything that had grown problematic for me. On another occasion I announced that if she ever got together with him, she'd probably live longer with him than she had with me. Again and again I had to give voice to all my fears, I had to conjure up all the things I least wanted to happen. She watched my face, pinched, enraged and hurt. I stood emptying the dishwasher and slammed the cupboard doors, as I talked. But in the next moment I'd go on about her having to be free, having to do what she wanted. As long as she was my wife and lover, I said, she could do what she wanted with anyone. I stood in front of her, blotchy-faced, glassy-eyed, manic. And all she wanted was to be left in peace.

And now she was coming home late again. Perhaps she was being flippant, she thought, perhaps she was being neglectful of us, of our relationship, but it couldn't be helped. She looked at his hands, Gunnar's hands on the wheel. Smooth, hairless, tanned. She wanted to tell him, that she felt she'd been neglectful again. But then he turned to her and said: *I've always liked to go skiing on my own. But now I prefer it when you're with me.*

She knew what this meant. She knew what her response should be. She heard herself respond, and her own words moved her. The heat shot through her body in waves. He drove on, she stared out of the window, not daring to look at him. He said something, without looking at her, precisely what she hoped he would say.

Some days earlier I'd called her at her work, I was in tears, she could barely understand what I said. She'd tried to calm me down, she suggested I go out, go skiing perhaps, and I'd answered that it wouldn't help. I'd already been out skiing, I'd taken the same route she usually took, with Gloveman. I could think of nothing else. I'd gone as fast as I was able, skied as hard and as far as I could, trying to exhaust myself. It helped to tire myself out, I stopped thinking. But as soon as I got back home I thought again about her and him.

I said we had to meet up, that I had to speak with her right away. She relented, she said she could go out to lunch. I sat in the car outside her office, we went for a drive, I started to talk, then I started to cry. I pulled over, she listened to me. I said that I couldn't go on, that it was torture, I was just waiting for what might happen, that she'd sleep with him, that she'd lose control over herself, over everything that was happening. That our family would be wrecked. What would become of me then, and what would happen to the kids? I hit the steering wheel, I hit my own face, I hyperventilated, I sobbed and curled up in my seat. She put her hands on me, that usually helped.

She told me to lean forward and breathe calmly. She made her voice gentle, intimate, comforting. It helped a little. Eventually she grabbed my shoulder and said *OK fine. I swear there won't be anything between him and me other than friendship. I guarantee it, does that help?*

And it did. It was as though, she thought later, she had switched on the light. I stopped crying, and turned to her with the look she knew and liked. My voice returned to normal, warm and deep. I drove her back to work, and when she was about to go in, I asked her to wait a moment.

– What you said was lovely, it was all I needed. But I don't want you to guarantee me anything. What kind of life would that be for you, or even for me? I want you to be alive. I want you to be free. I don't want you to give me any lifetime guarantees. I've suddenly grown so afraid of losing you. I wonder if I've always been afraid of it. But it's precisely this fear that could ruin everything between us. Isn't it? In Shakespeare's plays, it's his characters' desperate attempts at avoiding disaster that lead them right to it. They try to save themselves or others, and in so doing bring about the very thing they fear. The problem is not whether you are in love with him or not, what's dangerous is that I've become so afraid of it.

She reached over to me, trying to feel what she'd felt before. She saw her own hand on my shoulder, embraced me and released me, almost without thinking, her thoughts were elsewhere.

Their trips got longer and more frequent. He dropped her off at the gate. The house looked dark, she couldn't see anyone at the windows. She leaned forward to say goodbye. She closed her mouth and eyes, felt his cheek against hers. She breathed in his smell, the cool, fresh odour of speed and physical exertion and new snow. But something else too: a grown man's body, an exciting bitter heat that rose from beneath his clothes. He kissed her lightly on the cheek, a dry but promising kiss. He said *good luck*, and then she saw his hand on her knee. She hadn't felt it until she saw it. In that instant she felt an intense heat radiating up from his hand, up over her thigh. It went straight into her, through the whole of her, out to the tips of her fingers. She laid her hand on his for a moment, then she had to go.

The front door wasn't locked. She put her skis in the hallway, took off her boots as quietly as she could. She walked softly and calmly into the light. I wasn't in my usual place in the kitchen. She knew by the silence in the house that the kids were asleep. Our youngest boy breathed deeply and audibly, the door to the oldest was closed. The ceiling light was on, and a pile of papers lay on the kitchen table.

She called my name but there was no answer. She glanced through the papers, they were the plans of the house. What would I be doing with those? Then she heard me, I was coming up from the basement, up the spiral staircase that we'd been so proud of when we had it installed, white and smooth like a skeleton. She saw me as I climbed through the vertebrae, dark and ominous against the white.

We looked at each other, she said *Hi, I was a bit late after all*. She didn't get an answer to that either. I said

I hadn't heard her come in. She thought I looked quite happy, perhaps she could relax. I was, after all, the person she always confided in, even about Gunnar. She told me a story he'd just told her. He'd received a call from a man who'd been a former neighbour. They'd had a couple with kids living next door to their previous house. They used to chat over the fence, sometimes they had dinner at each other's houses, their kids played together. One day the neighbour's wife had put her hand on Gunnar's cheek, in front of everybody. She'd stroked his face, and then left. They'd had no contact with each other since Gunnar and his wife had moved here. But now this old neighbour, the man, had rung Gunnar to tell him that they were getting a divorce, and that their break-up was Gunnar's fault. His wife, he said, thought about nothing but Gunnar and it couldn't go on. That was the story. And she laughed as she told it, just as she had with Gunnar. But I just stared at her, shaking my head as though I didn't understand.

— That's a weird story.

— Yes, isn't it?

— There's something that doesn't quite fit. Don't you see? There's something missing in this story. What did he do to her?

— Nothing, they were just neighbours.

— So Gloveman is someone that everyone just simply falls in love with? It's beyond his control?

— I didn't say that.

— But that's what he's said. That was probably what he wanted you to hear, don't you think?

– He just told me about something that had happened to him.

– But what do you think he said to her? When they talked, this woman and Gloveman, what sort of conversations do you think they had? Do you think he talked to her in the same way as he talks to you?

– No, I don't think so.

– But imagine if he did. Imagine if he had just as close a relationship with her as he has with you, and then he just went off. Maybe they slept together, or maybe he simply got the confirmation he needed from her, and that was enough. Why did they move, do you know?

– They've got three children, they needed more space.

– Is that all? Are you sure?

She regretted telling me, she'd only meant to share an amusing little anecdote with me. It also occurred to her that she might have brought a certain slant of her own to the story, a certain pride in Gunnar, in his being a man that other women fell for. Why shouldn't she share that with me? After all, I wanted her to share everything. But now she decided she couldn't tell me about Gunnar any more, it had taken a completely wrong turn. She didn't want to hear another word about him from me. She pointed at the documents on the table, and said

– What are you doing with those?

– It's a floor plan of the house.

– I can see that.

– I thought we'd need it if we're going to talk to an agent.

– An agent?

— An estate agent.

— Are you thinking we should sell the house?

— I think we should go far away and start again. Do you remember we talked about living in the Lofoten Isles for a year? I think we should do it. As soon as possible, actually.

— The Lofotens?

— Yes, or even further north perhaps. Finnmark, Svalbard. You'll like it. You can go skiing as often as you like. You can walk in the mountains, climb. I'd like to start too, in fact.

— But my job is here.

— You can get a job anywhere. You're a doctor.

— But I like my job here.

— I know.

— I know you know.

— I'm not sure why you started working behind a desk.

— You encouraged me.

— I encourage you in whatever you want. But now we've got to get out of here.

— Why?

— To save our love. Our life. The family.

— Surely things aren't that bad.

— I'm afraid so.

— But need you be so afraid?

— You won't stop seeing him. You won't be able to.

— Do I have to stop seeing him? We're just good friends.

— You're attracted to him. You fancy him.

— Yes, I know I've said that.

— And he wants you.

— I can't be sure of that. And neither can you.

— He wants you, that's obvious. And you want him. And I want you to be free, to do what you want, with whoever you want, you know that.

— But suddenly that's no longer valid?

— You're my wife and lover. I don't want you to stop being that.

— I've not said that I want that to stop.

— No?

— No.

— I'm worried that you're not in control of the situation. You don't know what you're doing.

— I've got a new friend. A friend. Oughtn't it be possible — between the two of us more than any — for me to have a friend who just happens to be a man?

— Absolutely. But I no longer recognise you. You're never here with me these days. I'm frightened that everything's going to fall apart, don't you understand?

— I can't quit my job. I can't move.

— Why not?

— I want him in my life.

She said it, and she felt her eyes start to smart, the surface of her face start to burn, her hands, her toes, her knees, her groin, her earlobes start to burn. She let the tears run, it was like pissing on yourself, or like vomiting. She cried, she didn't turn away, didn't dry her face, just continued to look at me as the tears ran.

I got up and walked away, I leaned on the kitchen worktop and turned towards her and said

— is that how it is?

and she said

— yes

and I said

— you won't stop?

and she said

— I can't,

and I said

— you won't stop seeing him? Whatever it leads to?

and she said

— I can't,

and I said

— Okay, then I have to surrender, I have to find a way to hold out,

and she said

— does it have to be so difficult?

and I said

— but have you thought about how this will end?

and she said

— what do you mean by how it will end?

and I said

— what will happen to us, to you and me, and between you and him, have you thought about it? If you like him so much, where will it end? How will things be between us in the end?

And then she said, in a toneless voice, unwillingly, she noted it herself:

— No, I have not.

She doesn't want to think about such discussions now, why would she, she wants to move on, still they come back to her, out of nowhere. She'll be sitting in the car, running up a staircase, staring into her computer at work, and my face will suddenly appear before her. The thought of my face. And she'll remember something we said, the way I leaned towards her, my voice when it grew harsh and fearful. There was something in my eyes that would never relent. She wanted to avoid my gaze, to look away, but couldn't. I was her husband, her lover, the man she lived with. Everything hinged on the fact we had once met and fixed each other's gaze. And because of that she sat there and absorbed the fury and despair that I'd built up in all those hours that we were apart, until in the end it subsided, burned itself out and faded.

She remembers how I sat down in the chair and turned away. I wiped my hand over my face, again and again, I wanted to tear it off, to leave my old face behind and go on without it. She remembers all this, sees it before her, hears our voices within that room that no longer exists. My voice that hounds her and never lets up, the voice that goes on arguing, brutal and relentless in its insistence that everything I fear is true. And she tries to maintain a distance. Her voice grows lighter, more breathy and less resonant, she can barely hear herself. *No, it's not like that. No, why do you say that? No, no, I don't know, no.*

She remembers it, remembers it all, puts a hand over her eyes, and then lets it pass, lets it sink to the bottom, and forgets it again.

A two-storey house, in a neat row of other identical houses. A quiet street. Black-stained timber walls. White foundation walls and window frames. A red front door, which she often misses. She liked to come home, it looked as though the house was in the middle of a forest, a fairy-tale house. Though the door wasn't arched on top, and the house wasn't really in the middle of a forest. At the back was a little garden with gnarled old fruit trees. The trees were much older than the houses, they were originally planted as part of a huge orchard belonging to one big farmstead. The district got its name from this farmstead. The local school and shopping centre were also named after it, long after its demolition.

These terrace houses had been built in the 1960s, and now it looked as if the trees had been planted within the fences: four little trees in each little garden. One of the trees in our garden had a strong, low-hanging branch, perfect for a swing. In fact the previous occupants had made one. A raw plank of wood with two coarse ropes, the kind of swing you'd imagine in a sun-glinting dream of childhood. Our children often sat there, stretching their legs with their chubby bare knees. And whenever they sat on the swing, they'd start to sing. First the older one, then the next. Each summer and all summer one of our children would sit on that swing and sing, all through the years, it seemed, for as long as the little dream of our family lasted.

And now she had come home, and I had waited for her, and I had said *What will happen to us?* and *How do you think this will end?* She couldn't think about it, couldn't talk about it, needed to keep it to herself, and she said

– Shouldn't we just go to bed?

and I said

– Do you want to?

and she said

– Yes, please, I'm so tired.

And so we did, we got undressed together and got into bed together and lay side by side. We couldn't sleep. She turned to me and stroked my cheek, she put her arms round my neck. She felt my hand on her hip, she moved closer to me and then we started again, those gentle sounds, the murmuring and laughter and whispers, and she lay on her back, and I lay on top of her, and she said

– do you want to?

and I said

– yes

and she said

– come on then

and I said

– all right

and then she heard me say

– our hearts must never close.

Could I really have said that? Like a refrain from a second-class pop song, she was sure I had, and it said something about just how far things had gone with us, with me, and she said

– no

and then she said

– yes

and then she said

– I love you!

even though she thought she shouldn't have said it, not now, but still she said it, and we both said it, we yelled it into each other's faces, shouted it so it might be true again and she put her arms around my back and hands on my neck. She clawed at my back, felt with her nails for any unevenness in my skin. She heard me say something, but for her my voice had melted away. She felt her pulse beating in her ears, as though a carpenter was somewhere in the house banging a hammer on the walls. A moment later she must have fallen asleep. She was woken by the lamp going out, and by my lifting her thigh. She felt me enter her again, and she heard me say how lovely she was, how lovely it had been between us, that I wanted her one more time. My voice was warm in her ear, I was confident and sure, I was no longer fearful. She had made me feel safe, or we had made each other feel safe. I asked if she'd had a good ski trip, and she said she had. I wanted her to tell me about it, she told me where they'd gone, how far away it was, how lovely and how tranquil. She described the sound of their skis, the fresh fallen snow, the ski tracks, the moonlight, the shadows of the trees in the ice-blue snow. She heard me ask who had gone first, and she knew where I wanted to take this. She said that in the beginning he'd gone first, and that she'd watched him. I asked if she thought he was handsome, and she said yes, he was handsome, he held himself well, he was strong and walked with a fine rhythm. I moved inside her, she heard herself breathing and heard me say that I could see him before me, his back, his back on top of her. I said that I knew it would happen, it had to happen, there was no other way, one day she would lie as she lay now, on her back in bed with him on top of her. She heard me say that I wished I could be there then, that I could see her then, see her hands on his bare back as he lay on top of her.

— That's just something you say, she said.

— Yes, I said. But I do see it, and I know it's going to happen.

— You won't be able to tolerate it.

— I will. As long as I know that you're mine, you can do anything.

— I don't believe that one bit.

— Wait and see, it'll happen.

— You really believe it? You'd offer me up to him?

Et cetera, et cetera. She doesn't want to think about it any more. But she can't stop thinking about it. About how she lay under me in the dark and imagined herself elsewhere, in another bed, with another man, with him. And how when we had both come, I no longer wanted to talk about him, that it was as if he had suddenly ceased to exist, and this troubled her in a way that she couldn't even understand herself. All I wanted was to hold her close, to lie with my face in her neck.

Fortunately I fell asleep after that, and slept through the night without waking her. The following day we both got up, she took a shower, I woke the kids and we had breakfast. The kids went to school, first the youngest, then the oldest, then the house was empty, apart from the two of us. She was nervous I'd start to question her. She needed to go, she got ready, put on the dark green skirt that reached just above the knee, and the white blouse that was too tight across the shoulders. She knew it did something to me, though that was no longer her reason for choosing it. She put on some eyeliner, just a touch, so faint it was almost invisible, but it gave her confidence. I stood and watched her.

– Are you going to meet him today?

– I'm just having a coffee with him after work.

– You're making yourself nice for him.

– I'm only trying to look my best. As usual.

– Yes, but now you're doing it for him.

– Have you got a problem with that?

I shook my head. My eyes were glassy. She had to rush out. She pushed me gently aside, went to find her bag, her phone, everything she needed. I followed her, I hadn't shaved yet, hadn't taken a shower, my hair was sticking out like a bush on one side of my head, evidence of which side I'd slept on.

– Will you get together with him, d'you think?

– That's not a scenario we need to contemplate.

– Scenario? I don't understand what you mean.

– I don't think it'll happen.

– You know, you don't need to lose me if you get together with him.

– I don't think you could handle it.

– What won't I handle?

– Not being number one for me.

– Number one?

– Yes.

– Would I be number two?

– Yes.

I stood and looked at her, a book in one hand and a glass in the other. My face was red and blotchy, as though I'd been slapped. She thought: I need to go now before this goes too far, otherwise it might take all day. She said:

– I feel so much affection for you, Jon.

And that was wrong, of course, she shouldn't have said it, she shouldn't have used that phrase, she realised that instantly. She watched the colour drain from my face, and then return almost immediately. She could see I was irritated, or agitated, as though I'd gone into meltdown and was trying to pull myself back together. I threw my book on the floor, went to the sink and emptied the glass, set the glass down, too hard. I said something about it not helping if she pitied me. She said she really *had* to leave for work now. It was as if our jobs meant nothing to me any more, as if I was hell-bent on creating a drama, beyond which nothing else existed. Not that she could say that, of course.

We stood and looked at each other.

She took her bag and scarf.

And then, as so often before, my face somehow softened.

I went over to her and gave her a hug. She returned it, she felt me kiss her cheek. A little too wet for her liking. She looked up at me, I was taller than her, though not as tall as him, and the difference surprised her. But she mustn't think about that now. I drew her close and said in her ear

– I know you love me,

and then I let her go, almost pushing her away, so as to look into her face, I suppose. And she couldn't answer.

She didn't know what to say. She looked back at me, then nodded, and put on a bright smile. It was all she had to offer me. And then she left. I stood holding the door so she couldn't close it behind her. But she walked as fast as she could, she did not want to turn and look at me.

She thinks about it, then thinks about it no more. She gets up and goes to the window, it is dark outside, she sees her own face reflected in the glass. She remembers one evening towards the end of what had once been our life together, just before we ceased to know each other. She had heard a noise coming from the bathroom, she opened the door and saw me leaning over the sink crying. I gazed up at myself in the mirror. It looked, she remembers, as though my face had been torn apart, she stood a moment and watched me, the tears ran, snot ran, spittle ran, I gasped gurgled wailed and wept like a child, she thought, but as I stood there I stared into my own eyes. She recalls that moment, she sits and thinks it over for an instant, then gets up and goes out of the room, and remembers it no more.

10

A CONVERSATION WAS TO TAKE PLACE IN THE cold light of day, in an office, or in the waiting room outside an office, we sat side by side waiting to go in, we couldn't get up and leave, so we could finally talk.

– What happened to us, do you understand it?

– One day you suddenly pulled away from me, you wouldn't touch me, couldn't talk. It was like some awful illness, this love of yours, it came so suddenly and turned everything upside down.

– For me it was as though I was suddenly well. And I hadn't even known I was sick, because I liked my life with you. I thought I was happy, if that word can still be used. But shortly after I met him, I turned and looked again at what had been my life.

– And the thing that was missing was him?

– I don't have to answer that.

– I remember one night you were standing at the window smiling to yourself, and I asked what you were smiling about. I knew, but I had to ask anyway. You said you were just thinking. You didn't want to tell me more, but continued to smile, somehow secretively. You probably wanted to show me that something wonderful had happened to you. And the wonderful thing was that you were freeing yourself from me.

– I don't remember that.

– You wanted to show me how in love you were.

– You were the closest person to tell.

– A little later your phone rang. You went into the bathroom to take it. I heard your voice, heard you talking to him in there, for just over an hour.

– I was ruthless with you.

– Yes.

– It was inevitable.

– I'm glad you used that word.

– What? You mean *ruthless*?

– Yes, it helps me to hear you say it.

– I understand. But.

– But?

– But you know ...

– What? Oh yes, you're thinking that it's not really you saying these things.

– Well, it isn't. You're putting words in my mouth. You're imagining that I'm sitting here talking to you. You just make me say what you want.

– Not what I want, I've tried that, it doesn't work. I can't get you to say anything other than what I think you would have said if you were really here. But it helps to imagine it. To hear you say it.

– So what is it that you wish I would say?

– That I'm not able to make you say?

– Yes.

– Sorry perhaps.

– Isn't sorry too easy, Jon? And what should I really apologise for?

– For letting it happen? And for not knowing enough about yourself to see what you were doing, together with him, so that it looked as though you had no choice in the end.

– In the end, I had no choice.

– Exactly. And I wish you could apologise for that, Timmy.

– Isn't there something you're forgetting?

– You mean my part in everything that happened? You mean I should have let you be, I should have put up with you suddenly being *hopelessly and madly in love*? Yes, I should have. I'd prepared myself for something like that to happen, you and I had both prepared ourselves for years, even though we didn't realise it, so I should have held out and waited for it to pass. It might have taken a long time, a year, several years perhaps, before this infatuation released you. But I ought to have held out. We'd have been the kind of couple who each live their separate lives. Lots of people do, despite everything. You'd have been at home less, you'd have travelled more frequently and further away. He'd have come to pick you up and given you lifts home. The neighbours would have got used to seeing his car. The kids would have got to know about him. Everyone would have guessed what was going on, although few would have thought it through to its conclusion. And we'd have stopped talking about it. It would have been a tacit agreement between us. I wouldn't have expected so much from you. We'd have slept with each other less often. We'd have stopped kissing, apart from when something extraordinary happened. Little kisses, like a friendly pat on the shoulder. We'd have lived our own lives, with different interests and different friends. I'd probably have gone a bit to seed, but many men do. I'd have worn my old summer jacket too late into the autumn, and my winter jacket too late into the spring. I'd have overeaten, worn downtrodden shoes, waited too long for a haircut and taken less care of myself. My wilful self-neglect would lose its charm. And then I'd have started taking more exercise, like you, to compensate for the humiliation. Or perhaps I wouldn't even see it as a humiliation. Love is about power, and power relations shift continually, even between two people living together. Sooner or later I would also have fallen in love, an easy, mild, non-committal love, to restore the balance. No doubt I'd have met someone at a writers' workshop. Somebody with short hair and dainty glasses, who smelled of expensive moisturiser and wore a short, grey cashmere golfing cardigan. One of those deliciously soft cardigans! Whenever she stretched, the little cardigan would have ridden up, exposing her pale naked midriff. And whenever I put my arms around her, she'd have nestled against me devotedly, as I never knew you to. I could have lived like that, I could have been her reliable, friendly lover. An adult, sensible relationship, a kind of simple happiness, seen from outside. Although I wouldn't have let it go that far, I'd have been too ambivalent, I would have gradually extricated myself. I'd never tell you about her, we'd no longer share things like that. And if you'd stayed together with Gloveman, sooner or later you'd have come home after a row with him. And I'd have been there, as always. I'd have noticed there was something about you, and hopefully I'd have understood that you needed space. You would have taken a bath, eaten chocolate, unusual for you. Then you might have sat down beside me, without saying a word, and I'd have held you, also without a word. You might have fallen asleep perhaps, with your head on my shoulder, and then woken up not knowing which of our two shoulders you were resting on. And sooner or later I'd have felt your hand on me again, that warm touch on my neck as we were driving. Or on my forearm, when you wanted to hold me back to tell me something. I'd still have thought about what that hand had been used for, all those times you were with him and not me. But perhaps you would start to miss what you and I had together, how we used to flirt with each other through other people, how we believed that we'd create another kind of life. Or was I the only one who believed it, that we could create something that nobody else had come near? It was all much simpler and more pragmatic for you. But still. If I'd not been so fearful, so desperate and so agitated, if I'd just let you do what you wanted with him for one or two or three years, then you would doubtless have come back and become the person you were before, with me, don't you think? And wouldn't we then have lived with a more mature kind of love, a more moderate and realistic tenderness? Our confidence, once shattered, could be gradually rebuilt. And our faces, ravaged by life, would gradually look more worn, softer and kinder than before. I see our faces turning to each other with a strange kind of resignation, a more composed and gentle curiosity. Don't you think? And couldn't this life have been stronger than the first we tried? Mightn't that have been a possible life for the two of us? Why don't you answer?

11

SOME WEEKS AFTERWARDS SOMETHING HAP-
pened to me. Something took form in the dark, in my
body, as I slept. Our older son was the only one who noticed it, and he told nobody. Timmy and I had recently left
each other, that was how we put it, we each lived in the
house every other week now, and this was my week with
the kids. I was home, it was evening, my youngest boy was
asleep, and the eldest was in his room at the computer. He
was playing *The Sims*, but he had his door open, unusually,
because he wanted to keep an eye on me.

He sat watching me clear the fridge, throwing out old
food. I let any food stay that I had bought myself. And
I didn't remove any food Timmy had recently bought.
But anything we'd bought together when we were still a
couple, still married, I took off the shelves and threw away.
Pots of mustard and tubes of Kalles Kaviar, jars of olives
and anchovies, taco sauce and mango chutney, a greasy
jar of sun-dried tomatoes, cloudy capers, dehydrated jam,
a mouldy tub of low-fat sour cream, cans of beer and a
wrinkly salami sausage, shrunken lemons and the corpse
of a lettuce that was brown at the edges. I also threw away
an unopened jar of honey, several tubes of mayonnaise,
untouched tins of tuna and a whole pack of hot-smoked

salmon. I threw away everything that had been there from before. I eradicated our old life. I filled one rubbish bag after the other, tied them up and took them outside to throw them away. The heavy plastic lid of the bin shut with a resounding thud outside, harsh, intransigent, as our son listened on. But I must have felt better afterwards, since I sang as I walked back in. He disliked it intensely, that I sang and that I was throwing out food that had been our family's food. It put me on the wrong side, I was accelerating the violent changes to our family. I was obviously eager to forget everything that had been, and for that he despised me.

The moment I'd started clearing the fridge, he'd come out and asked what on earth I was doing, and why I was throwing away our food. I told him there was too much old stuff, and the fridge needed a clean. He watched me as I proceeded to dispose of everything we used to put out on the table for breakfast or supper in the life that had been ours. A tin of pâté that no one had ever eaten, that had never been opened, but that we *always* put out on the table, that *had* to be put on the table for his world to be stable, as he needed it now, more than ever. I sorted the old from the new with rapid, insensitive gestures. I failed to understand his objection, his rage, his despair. He stood and watched me, felt a burning sensation behind his eyes, the nauseating throb of his pulse in his ears. He cleared his throat loudly, but I carried on. I shoved my arm deep into the fridge and pulled something out that had frozen to the back, I turned towards him with a shrivelled pepper that looked like the wrinkled heart of a small animal,

I asked if he wanted it, I meant it as a joke, but he shook his head in disgust.

He went into his room and closed the door. He slammed it hard, his eyes filled with angry tears, though I clearly didn't notice that either. A bit later it went quiet in the kitchen. He started to wonder what I was doing. Perhaps I'd started clearing out everything else that belonged to our old life, perhaps I was sitting there deleting pictures. He emerged from his room, pretending he wanted to watch TV. But I was sitting at the kitchen table, reading a book, I'd poured myself some red wine into a small kitchen glass. I looked up and smiled ruefully at him. He disliked that too, the new smile I'd adopted since the divorce. It was he who called it *the divorce*, despite the fact formalities were still incomplete. He loathed the word and said it as often as he could, pronouncing it as two sharply distinct sounds, *dee* and *vorce*. He made it sound like an appalling mistake, and it was, especially for him. Our family had been cracked open, everyone we knew could look inside, or thought they could. He was ashamed of us. He looked at me, hunched over my book, motionless, almost as though I were asleep. Suddenly I looked up at him and asked if he was hungry and whether we should perhaps eat something together. He refused politely, he'd eaten a burger on the way home, but he didn't want to tell me that.

He sat in front of the TV and watched me go to the fridge again. There was only one thing I hadn't had the heart to throw away, and that was a bowl of leftover risotto. He knew why: these were the remains of the last meal I'd made for her. She'd been away on a work trip, and when she came home late that night, I was waiting with her dinner. There was nothing unusual in that, it was what followed that was unusual. We sat at the table and talked, and very calmly we ended our relationship. She cried a little, not much. A few tears rolled down her face and fell into her food. I'd cried so much already – he'd heard and seen it frequently over the past year – so he presumed that I'd finally become cold and resolute. Afterwards she went to bed in the spare room and I tidied up. I put the leftovers in a little bowl on the top shelf in the fridge, and since then the bowl had stood there.

That was three weeks ago.

The bowl contained large swollen grains of rice, cooked in white wine with Italian porcini, crispy bacon, beetroot, thyme, grated Parmesan. Now I scraped the crusty leftovers into a pan and heated them. He sat with his face turned towards the television, but continued to follow my every move. He saw me continue to throw away food that I found in the cupboards. Seed mixes, packets of raisins, torn bags of flour and half-empty packets of biscuits. Even unopened packets of crisps and peanuts were binned, simply because they belonged to our old life. He decided he would get the bags of crisps and peanuts out of the bin the next day. He would fetch everything out and put it back in the cupboards as soon as Monday came and I moved back out. The remains of our divorce-supper were the only food I'd saved, and weirdly I now wanted to eat them. He watched me stir the rice in a frying pan until it was hot and soft and golden again. I ate straight from the pan standing at the worktop. It seemed such a demonstrative gesture. So uncharacteristic. He moved to another chair so he wouldn't have to watch. He was slowly drawn into what was on the screen, a documentary about religious sects in the USA. A former member of the Scientologist Church was saying she would never be herself again. She'd been made to believe her old life was empty, but now she longed to return to what had once been normal and ordinary. He turned up the sound, wanting me to hear what she said. Her words took on another meaning for us, here in these rooms, right now. He heard me rinse the frying pan and wash it under hot running water. He had no idea how, but he knew I'd left remnants of food in the sink. I'd always been the one who insisted that the sink should be cleared of any bits, rinsed out and wiped dry. I'd always been the one to clean up after Timmy and the kids whenever they didn't do it properly. Now I was just leaving it, and he had a feeling that was how I intended to go on. Crumbs, left-over yogurt, tea leaves, from now on I'd leave them all in the sink, just as she always had. He saw through me, he saw I was trying to be like Timmy had been, as if that could help us now.

Later that evening he saw me lying in bed with all my clothes on and the duvet pulled up halfway over me. I'd dropped off. I no longer closed the bedroom door, the way she and I always had. I lay in the middle of the bed, as though my body had fallen from a great height. The light was still on. He disliked that, the door being left open so he had to see me lying there on his way to the bathroom. And the fact that I hadn't gone to bed properly, I probably hadn't even brushed my teeth, he felt my toothbrush and it seemed dry. He came in and turned off the reading lamp above my head. I didn't wake up. He closed the door, went into the kitchen and fried an egg. On his way to bed, he opened my bedroom door again. I had turned over and was lying on my side. I'd obviously got undressed. He saw my face in the light from the hall, yellow, like an oriental mask, a face that depicted eternal grief, and I was sleeping with my mouth open.

Two weeks later I had begun to change physically. I had grown thinner, my cheeks were sunken and my cheekbones dominated my face. But it seemed to him that I was pleased about this. One afternoon I punched a new hole in my belt with a kitchen knife, I said I needed to buy new clothes, I'd gone down two sizes. I was cultivating this, that was clear, I felt both sorry for myself and simultaneously pleased, which upset him even more. He was in despair over me, I seemed completely unaware of what was really happening to me. The problem, he realised, lay in the fact that we used organic arborio rice specially imported from a small Italian producer. Mixed in it there had been some minuscule grains of unpolished rice. These grains had gone into the packet just as they'd grown in the field, husks and all. It wouldn't take many, perhaps just a couple of these tiny grains. They'd sat on the extreme edge of the wok as I made the risotto, and maybe looked like pieces of hot golden onion, so that I didn't turn them with the spatula or stir them into the bottom of the pan. They'd remained uncooked and unconsumed, first on the top of the risotto and then at the bottom of the leftovers dish. It was also possible that I'd kept the food that was left on her plate too, and that the salt in her tears might have released a chemical reaction. He'd read articles online about life under the ice on alien planets, about new diseases appearing in the guts of people who ate genetically modified food. The unpolished grains of rice could easily have been transferred to the bowl of leftovers, which I'd heated up and shovelled into my mouth, straight from the pan. I'd eaten the whole lot, even those two lonely grains of rice that came untreated from the rice fields of Genoa: tiny capsules of life, just waiting for the chance to germinate.

As early as that first night, when he saw me lying asleep with a yellow face and open mouth, the young seedlings must have attached themselves to the thin lining of my stomach. They'd taken root and begun to sprout, and a few days later tiny rice plants had started to spread in the warm, moist environment. Delicate green strands wound their way into the dark pit of my stomach, stealing all the nourishment that should have been mine. Organic life forms primarily take their nourishment from other life forms, as we know, and now my stomach offered the perfect habitat for a minuscule grain of rice.

He took a picture of me and showed it to his mother, eager to hear what she'd say. She and I hardly met these days – every Monday one of us would leave in the morning, and in the afternoon the other would come home. We each stayed with friends in the week we were away, and he wanted her to see the state I was in: gaunt, hyper, touchy and febrile. I had my back to the window in his photo, it was dark behind me and I stared into the camera with big, serious eyes. He hoped she would be shocked and take the initiative to meet me, that it might change things between us. But she just glanced quickly at the picture and commented that I'd let my beard grow. She had no idea, of course, that I was walking about with sprouting rice fields in my stomach.

Even I was unaware of the fact I had laid myself vulnerable to an alien life form. Though I may have had some idea about it, he thought, because he noticed that I studied myself in the mirror more frequently than before. My eyes were now deep in their sockets, and the surrounding skin was darkening like old handbag. An angry-red eczema had developed on my eyelids. I was no longer just his father, I'd become a solemn, hollow-cheeked man who had lost his woman to another man. The mere thought of it was embarrassing. I often came into his room wanting to talk about life, about what I thought was *our* life, *our* family life, but which in truth only concerned me. He had to protect himself from me. He developed a sense of humour to hold me at a distance, calling me the Thin Man, the Skeleton and the Old Geezer. Yet we sometimes laughed more freely than before. He also saw his mother more clearly, now that he no longer saw her as part of the hermetically sealed couple she and I had been. She'd sit with him in the evenings after his little brother had gone to bed, she'd watch the movies he wanted to see, something she'd never done before. He noticed that she had to cover her eyes with her hand every time someone on the screen got shot or suffered abuse. He felt sorry for her, her hair had gone a different colour at the roots, he'd never seen that before. He looked at her neck, and he thought she looked lonely and rather comical. She was a middle-aged woman who'd fallen in love with another man, she'd destroyed everything because of this infatuation. Now she wouldn't talk about the other man, the man I referred to as Gloveman. Things weren't right with her, that was clear.

He couldn't feel any pity for me, I should have been more careful, I shouldn't have let myself be humiliated. And of my own free will! He'd heard me declare it would be fine for his mother to have two lovers if she wanted. He could never forgive me for that. He realised that he had to look after his mother now, but had no idea how. He suggested she go to the hairdresser's and get her hair coloured again. He created an alternative family on *The Sims*, where she and I were still married, and we were still a family. He recreated the same rooms, with similar furniture, and we all had the same habits and routines. He made sure she still took exercise, but alone, and that I sat reading my books. He saw to it that we ate, that we tidied up after ourselves, that we slept at night and went to work in the morning. He was vigilant when it came to our earning money, nobody must go without. He watched as we talked together in excited or grumpy Simlish. He tried to get me to join in with his game, but I complained that I couldn't relate to my avatar, a man with thick slicked-back hair. He tried giving me thinner hair, bigger eyes, hollower cheeks, a longer nose, but I was never satisfied with any of the alternatives. One evening, when he'd left me on my own with the game for a few minutes, my avatar set fire to himself. I burned to death in the kitchen as I stood there frying food, and together we listened to my wild screams and the crackling sound of fake flames. But outside the game I gradually started to change again. After a few months the rice field in my stomach wilted, no doubt the seedlings died from the lack of light. I shaved every day again, and started to put on weight. I soon began to resemble the person I'd been.

And he disliked that too, my being myself again, just as though nothing had happened. He was shell-shocked and would be for years. He had no means of defence, he'd had a sheltered upbringing, nothing could have allowed him to predict what happened to us. He was the one who was supposed to change, not us.

12

BUT NONE OF THIS HAS HAPPENED YET. WE still live together in the same house, Timmy and I still sleep next to each other at night and presume we'll go on being lovers, despite any recent difficulties. It is March, a Friday night, everywhere bodies are dressing and undressing, in large rooms and small, but for us this night will never end, it will replay itself in the present ad infinitum: she goes back to the office after dinner. This is no longer an uncommon occurence. Two or three times each week she waits for this moment. She is sitting at the dining table, she has already checked her mail and the news several times, she closes her laptop, she straightens up and stretches lazily, hands above her head, just as always, and then says

   – I'll be off now.

and I answer, or rather, I don't answer this time, I just nod. She knows without looking at me that I'm falling apart inside. I am disappointed in her or despairing over myself, she doesn't know which and doesn't want to know, she tries to push it away. Ever since she sat down at the table, she's been waiting for the moment she can leave. She has kept an eye on the cooker clock, she has helped our youngest with his homework and whispered into his ear that he's the best boy in the world. He sits with his breast-bone pressed against the table's edge, something he's done this entire winter and spring. At every meal he sits at the table and watches us. Every single object that's placed on the tabletop creates a vibration, and sometimes our voices create discernible vibrations through the tabletop too, and he catches all these small tremors with his skeleton. He is serious and very focused, with his short, glossy hair and soft hands. She strokes our oldest son on the back of his neck as she passes, he's begun to pull away from any gesture of affection, but she needs to touch him even though he shakes her off.

At this moment she is the only person talking. Her voice doesn't sound as relaxed and intimate as she'd hoped. I'm standing by the kitchen worktop, I turn to her with my eyebrows raised, she notices the deep lines that run across my forehead that the children liked to count when they were small, standing with bare feet on my thighs, reaching up and tracing their fingers along each furrow. She remembers their pale infant-bodies, naked white bellies and nappy-clad bottoms, first one, then the second a few years later, their hair always falling into soft curls after they'd been bathed, one moment they were leaping into our bed, the next they had started school and soon half their childhood had gone. She is touched by these warm, happy thoughts, then she grows agitated and wants to cry.

It feels like a fever — has she gone insane, what is she actually doing? But she *must* go and meet him, she can't do otherwise. She inhabits two worlds. Just a few kilometres away he is moving around in his room, his hairless body, golden, smooth and lithe beneath his shirt, beneath the formal pressed trousers. She imagines him, the way he turns to her, the way he smiles and tilts his head, out of shyness perhaps or everything that's built up between them, the attraction, the affirmation, the thrill of it all. It's not true that their love has grown from nowhere, by chance, they've allowed it to grow, both of them, they've driven it on determinedly with each glance, each touch, every word they've said. And now they can no longer turn back, at a certain point an irreversible shift occurred: they feel greater loyalty to each other now than to anyone else. She does at least. He says he feels his pulse quicken each time he sees her name appear on his phone. He says she is everything he didn't know was missing in his life. Or he says something else perhaps, but every word he utters serves to strengthen her feelings, to raise her expectations. She lets herself be driven onwards by the urge to make it happen, the urge to go all the way, whatever the consequence. Might it have been like that? Yes, it must have been. Later when she tells people about it, it sounds alien and unreal, like a story she's made up. But now she is in the midst of it, she wants only this, nothing else, that is what she tells herself and him, and she releases her grip, lets herself fall into the warm darkness.

And I am standing in her way, it seems. I am concretely standing in front of her in the kitchen now, waiting for her to explain or defend her sudden determination to meet him again tonight. It will be the fourth evening this week. But there is no more to say, she thinks, she won't be held down. I turn away from her and continue to tidy up, moving about the kitchen with studied calm. No plate will be slammed down too hard on the worktop to make her think I am irritated. I have encouraged her in all this. It might even be said that I'm still striving to make it easy for her, though I'm not doing too well. Emotional baggage travels faster than sound between living bodies, and she doesn't even need to look into my face to know that this is not okay, that all is not well.

All those emotions she thinks she sees in me have surfaced in her before she even realises she's picked them up from me. She is impatient and gets up too abruptly, her voice sounds moody when she says *bye for now, then*. She regrets it, but she's already late. She closes the door a little harder than usual. She sits on the bench in the hall and pulls on her boots, boots that are almost knee-high, soft suede, she gets up and takes down her coat, shoves her arms in the sleeves, straightens her collar and does up the buttons. Three large, white frosted buttons, her fingers push them deftly through elaborately embroidered buttonholes. She watches herself in the mirror. She thinks of his gaze, how he'd have seen her now. Her coat is a light blue, neat and close-fitting with a thin belt at the waist. Not so close-fitting as to be too tight, she can't bear that, to feel restricted, but tight enough to make her feel good. On certain days, even now, she feels embraced as she buttons up this coat. She got it from me for Christmas, and she'll use it long after I've become her ex-husband, the man from whom she no longer receives gifts, not even for her birthday. Yet nothing about this coat reminds her of me, or what we called our love. She has many things she can't use because she got them from me: the short blue denim dress and the long grey cardigan, a pair of white jeans and almost all the jewellery she owns. She has stopped wearing jewellery. But she still wears this coat, it is somehow disconnected from me, even though I bought it for her. We gave each other expensive gifts that last Christmas, she tore off the paper and opened the box and found a sky-blue coat from an exclusive little boutique. She'd seen this coat herself just days before Christmas, in a shop I often went to when I looked for gifts for her, and in a momentary flash she hoped she might get it. And there it was, she held it up against herself and said, *it's amazing, so lovely*, and it sounded like something she might have said in the past, it wasn't quite right, and she felt it. Her mistake was to say anything she might have said a year ago. I got up and pulled the kids' presents out from under the tree, I straightened up, she could see I felt uncomfortable, that I was offended. My face closed, everything that was alive in me vanished, retreating far into my body becoming invisible to all.

Presumably I shall miss her forever, she thinks. My impending loneliness is inversely proportional to her own tremendous happiness. And she is filled with both tenderness and malice in ever-changing ratio, which frequently blends into just one feeling: love's last bitter offerings, frayed empathy, and grim tenderness not entirely well meant, in which every minor irritation fuses with her pity for me and desire to escape me without it looking like a betrayal.

We'd grown up together and we'd had children to confirm our love in new living flesh. A child is the final confirmation of love, even if that love proves short-lived, even if that love proves a fleeting physical attraction, or proves long-lasting but nonetheless lacking any deep foundation. Many people live together without any deep foundation, perhaps this was true, after all, of us? She had believed we were so deeply and closely bound, more than any other people we knew. But if this love came to an end, this would have retrospective power, we didn't realise that yet, but the reality was this: if our love ceased to exist one day, then it had never existed at all.

The kids were still there, of course, but they were no longer a confirmation of our love, we released them from that task. They would be like other children whose parents are divorced, thrown upon their own resources and our divided care. But they didn't know that, not yet, and neither did we.

Still standing on the steps outside our house, she throws a dark blue shawl round her neck, pulls it up over her mouth and feels the warmth of her breath. She closes the gate behind her and walks with hurried steps along the path. Snow, streetlamps, lighted windows in the houses. Her heart hammers behind her ribs. Her fingers curl up inside her mittens. Night is falling, but slumbering in the darkness is an indestructible metallic light. This light is about to wake from its sleep, she can sense it to her fingertips. Soon the snow will crumble, the evenings will grow longer, the grass will thaw in the gardens, as green as when the snows arrived. When she was a child some forty years ago, the grass always went yellow in the autumn, but now it stays green until it is decked in snow, and is still equally green when it reappears in April. These are the things she focuses her mind on now, so as to keep her excitement and anticipation at bay until she is far enough away from home. Soon the winter's grit will surface on grey asphalt, and soon all those objects that were thrown into the snow by mistake or in violent rage will be unveiled to all, blanched, miserable, shocking to the eye. Soon the call of the sparrow and great tit and thrush will be heard in the early morning, et cetera, et cetera. Soon it will be spring, soon summer, and what will happen to the two of us then? She dare not think about it, she thinks, though she thinks about it every second.

Two or three nights a week and every Sunday she goes back to the office to see him. The office is one of the few places they can meet, when they're not on one of their outings. They're planning another project together, and this time they're confident of getting management approval. It gives them the chance to work together at least. Hardly anyone works overtime in her department; besides, she can lock her door, nobody ever disturbs them. She generally leaves home after our youngest son has gone to bed, but sometimes earlier. It depends on whatever time suits Gunnar; he also has a family. He has children that need driving here or there, and a marriage that's still a marriage, at least on the surface. She doesn't know what he's said at home, perhaps nothing. She doesn't know what he thinks privately when he's alone. She doesn't know if he feels the same as her. Sometimes this puts her into a frenzy and she wonders *Is this happening only to me? Am I alone in this?* But come the evening, when he finally walks though the door of her office building, she sees the effect of her presence in his face. He takes a single step from the shadows into the light, and it is her own light she sees him in. She opens the door to let him in, they follow each other up the stairs, she walks ahead, and not before they enter the sketchily lit corridor does she stop and turn to look at him, finally allowing him to embrace her. Their faces seek each other. Human faces are so shockingly naked, easily read and expressive, and bodies search always for other bodies. And now it is she and he who have found one another, everything else disappears around them. He holds her. She holds him. They let go, step back to meet each other's gaze. Shining happiness, mutual attraction. Who could resist? Almost nobody, and certainly not her, not now. She leads him into the office. It's no secret that they meet, they are working together, that's what they have said, to families and colleagues. This evening they sit side by side in front of the screen, taking turns to use the keyboard. He moves his thigh close to hers, she presses her thigh against his. This has happened before, they frequently sit up close now, she knows I think this, they talk quietly, they laugh, they hold each other's gaze. These little intimacies have become the norm between them, there's no stopping now. And for a long time they've exchanged confidences about the everyday details of their lives, significant and otherwise, about their kids, about what they do when they're apart. Each of them remembers what the other said, asks how things went with the child who fell down the stairs, the kitchen tap that suddenly sprang a leak and the plumber who came and repaired the bathroom tap by mistake. And so from a distance, yet with almost domestic familiarity, they follow each other's lives. Their voices in that little office are hushed and intimate, they follow each other in pitch and intensity, they have started to resemble each other. Like a married couple, she thinks, as though they were already living together. Perhaps they've always been alike, it was an inexplicable stroke of luck that they, of all people, should meet each other now. Perhaps nothing would have happened if they hadn't looked into each other's eyes that little bit too long, she thinks later. Neither wanted to capitulate to the other, they drove each other on, their eyes refused to yield once locked. In both of them: an accelerated flow of blood through the very thinnest veins.

That night he suddenly puts his right hand over her left on the keyboard and lets it rest there. She stops talking. Feels his hand on hers. She can feel his pulse in his wrist, ticking against her skin like a minuscule organic clock inside his flesh. It is somehow moving, almost unbelievable that she can feel his pulse. He is talking, she has no idea what about, and she leans towards him as simultaneously he leans towards her. It's strange that it's never happened before, but they've resisted for almost a year, they have postponed this moment, and now it has come: she opens her mouth and meets his mouth, their lips are warm and dry, but the tip of his tongue is cold, she observes this, it strikes her that he must have been sitting with his mouth open, he's been tense, he has known this was coming, and now he finally locks his mouth around her mouth.

Timmy and Gunnar kiss. Their mouths suck tight to each other. His arms wrap around her, he draws her to him, his hands travel over her back, her hips, her waist, up to one shoulder, where her sweater has slipped down allowing him to touch bare skin. With his other hand he grabs her hip and pulls her closer, their office chairs bump a little disruptively into each other, he tries to get her to move across, to sit on his lap, but she doesn't want to, not yet. He has different clothes on today, a chequered shirt with a vest underneath. She has placed her hands on his back, one far up, just below his shoulder blade, the other lower on the small of his back. She feels his skin under his shirt, lets her fingertips drift up his spine, an unreal moment, the first time she's felt his bare skin under her own bare hands. She doesn't think of it until afterwards. A kiss that lasts an hour, a month, that could have lasted a lifetime. She breathes through her nose and answers him with her tongue, she can't stop herself from moaning, groaning, the sounds a body makes to welcome another. It makes him more confident, or more eager, he shoves his hand down the back of her waistband, he pushes his hand down a little further and drags her to him –

But enough now, the rest is inaccessible to her, and thereby inaccessible to me.

She draws a black curtain over what happens in the office that night. She lets it happen without seeing herself from the outside, and afterwards she forces herself not to think about it. Though of course she thinks about it anyway, there is a light coming from her, from within, it shines through her skin like a lantern in a far-off tent on an open plain. She has set forth on her journey now, she has walked away from her old life, left it behind her, and whatever happens to her now will permeate everything she does and says in the coming days. But she forces herself not to formulate the thought, to put it into words or sentences. She looks flushed and feverish and flurried. She loses things, forgets what she was going to say. She seeks solitude at every opportunity, sits gazing into thin air and smiling to herself.

She comes home late that night, later even than usual. She lets herself in quietly, pulls off her boots and hangs up her coat. The rooms are in semi-darkness and tidy, the kitchen tops attendant with their gleaming surfaces: the toaster stands alone, the coffee machine's tiny steadfast eye blinks, the slender bottles of certified olive oil and balsamic vinegar maintain their dignity, the soft lighting over the polished glass cooker top shines safe and harmonious, only a half-slice of mango sits on a plate with its black-speckled dark green back turned up. She carefully opens the doors to the kids' rooms to look at them. First the youngest, then the oldest. They are both asleep, their breath filled with sweetness. They are children, even the one who is so sure he isn't. He knows nothing now of what she knows. He sleeps on his back, his mouth half open, like the little boy he was, not so very long ago.

She goes into the bathroom, she tries to avoid her own gaze in the mirror, but has to look. Quickly, just a hurried, searching look into her own eyes: *What have I done, impossible to regret, such a rush of feelings, can't resist, how will it go, with what, with everything, who knows, I'll meet him tomorrow.*

She takes a shower, reluctantly, she doesn't want to wash him away, but it doesn't seem right to lie next to me without taking one first. She is washing him away so as to have him to herself in peace, she thinks to herself, so I won't come into contact with what she has of him with her. She brushes her teeth and moisturises herself, caressing her body with the lotion, thinking of his hands, and how he. Thinking of her own hands, and how she. And how they. No, she finishes in the bathroom quickly. All she wants is to sleep and to rest. And then she enters the darkness of our bedroom where I lie sleeping on one side of the bed. It's easier than you'd think to slip through the gaps, to go from one life to another. She has returned now for a fleeting moment to what was once her entire existence.

She lies down carefully on her side of the bed. As she sneaks in under the double duvet, she notices that I'm sleeping in a T-shirt and pants, she's pleased, it's just one more sign that our relationship has entered its final phase, even for me. We will no longer sleep naked together. She can barely hear me breathe. Imagine if I was dead now? Just like that? I might have had a stroke or heart attack, something fatal. Middle-aged men often die suddenly, and if I died now, she'd have no trouble mourning me. She could have been the quietly resigned widow, and simultaneously been joyously and ecstatically in love. It's a surprising thought; she understands now how someone might want to kill the person they live with, how they might suddenly see no other way out than to mix a poison or take a rifle and shoot them in the head, or strangle them with their bare hands, strangle this person with whom they were in bed, naked and relatively happy, just a few days prior. Because there is no other way to free oneself. The other must die in you, be defeated, erased. She must free herself from me, and she has already done so. In her interior life, which has become the only real life, I have already perished, I am vanquished. I fell away quite peacefully, I suddenly became unimportant, I drifted to the furthest edges of her life without knowing it.

But the hardest thing is that I *do* know. I have more than a passing suspicion. I follow her every move, register each inner change as it occurs in her, independently of anything she says. I have grown psychic. I find signs everywhere. That's the way jealousy works. It enables me to see everything, long before it happens. That's how it feels. And if I hadn't believed that I already knew everything about the two of them, she'd have been able to let the days pass and hope things might quietly resolve themselves.

She falls asleep alone, on her back, with one hand crossed over the other, as though she were ill. But she's not ill, she is healthier than before, she feels protected by what has happened, by what is to come. Everything that happens to her now is good, any changes are of the good sort.

Next morning she is friendly but remote, and manages to keep me at a distance. It's a Saturday, she tells me she needs to work with him again today, they have a deadline and there's something they must complete. Her tone is relaxed and direct, she only just manages to resist the temptation to hint at what she's really talking about. She says she hopes it's okay by me. She moves from room to room as she talks, making sure to avoid my gaze, expresses her needs without giving me a chance to interrupt. She detects resistance, reluctance, disappointment, whatever it is, but doesn't let it touch her, it is after all no longer relevant, now that she's living in another world, with somebody else.

She leaves and stays out all day, an agreed return time of three is moved to five, then seven, *it's taking so much time* and then to nine, *sorry, we're nearly finished!* She gets back home at nine thirty. She is with the children until they go to bed, and then she wants to go to bed too. She needs peace, to close her eyes, to return to her hyper-reality, to take strength from all that's new and life-changing. But she doesn't escape me, I'm lying in bed, on my side, fully clothed. For a moment she hopes I've fallen asleep. But then she notices that I'm crying, or that I have been crying, and lies down beside me. She strokes my face. She speaks to me softly, saying my name, she tries to soothe me, manages to soothe me, so that I stop sobbing. We lie there for a long time, side by side. She sleeps a little, wakes and realises that I get restless if she lies still for too long, and continues to stroke me. It feels safe, beautiful, intimate, even she thinks so. She is relieved that she didn't need to say anything. All in all, it is an advantage that I'd imagined this would happen long before it actually did. This way we can calmly and lovingly finish our relationship and help each other extricate ourselves with some dignity.

But then I turn towards her. I haven't fallen asleep, after all. I take her hand in mine, stroke the back of it, then her fingers. Once, a long time ago, I used to run my thumb and forefinger down the length of her fingers, one by one, from the base of each finger to its tip, as if I were pulling off a piece of fabric, as if I were undressing her hand, finger by finger. I start to do that now. I take her thumb first, then her index finger, and work my way to her little finger, first one hand and then the other. She used to like it, she used to ask me to do it, now she just waits for me to finish.

I say that she has beautiful hands, that I like to look at them, that I like to think of what she can do with them. She pictures what she's done with them, and waits for me to say it, that I've understood what has happened. But I say

– Think of all the things your hands have done with me. Some day you might do the same things with another man. I'd have liked to see that.

She watches me roll onto my back, pull my underpants down my thighs, I want her to touch me, or I want to touch myself while she looks on. She pushes herself away from me slightly. She thought we were finished with each other in that way, she thought I knew what had happened yesterday and today, she'd been certain that I would have noticed the change in her. All we could do now was to find a way to leave each other, quietly and in a civilised manner and with a sort of tender affection. Henceforth, we would be like brother and sister.

But I feel secure again now, because she is lying beside me, or because she has been lying here stroking my face with her hand. Or maybe because I can't really imagine that it could ever happen, this thing that has happened, the fact that she is no longer my love and lover – she cannot be, since I am not that for her.

Just a few days earlier I had said: Shouldn't we, the two of us, be able to get through this? Shouldn't I be able, I had said, to endure her falling in love with another? Who else could endure it, if not me? Who else, if not her, could fall head over heels in love outside marriage? Shouldn't our love survive this? Hadn't we always talked about everything that we found sweet or attractive or tempting? I had said all this, and she remembers how my voice came with my breath, erratic and intimate and loving words that slapped her in the face. We stood and held each other before she left home, kissing intermittently as I spoke, and in the end she asked if I thought she looked nice. She had put on some make-up, I teased her, saying she'd put it on for him. Afterwards she turned at the gate and waved. Our marriage was, she thought, unlike any other marriage she knew, but she is no longer sure what she meant by that.

She sits up, she wants to go out of the room, out of the house, she doesn't know what to say to me. A moment ago she thought how she would have liked to share it with me, this thing that has happened – this great joy, this burning passion. She hasn't been in love with anyone else since the time she fell in love with me, nearly twenty years ago. In truth she has never been so in love before, she concludes with an intensity close to rage. She wants to tell me, to tell me that she's never experienced anything like this, not even with me. Imagine, the woman who never believed she could fall in love with anyone else! Or perhaps, she's been waiting for this all along, perhaps she's been preparing herself for it in secret? In the future it will be impossible to believe otherwise. Another life has opened up. She wants to share it with me, because I am the obvious person to share it with. In fact it ought to be possible, she thinks, for us to talk calmly about it together, and possible even that I could share her great joy. I should be happy for her and share it with her, at a respectful distance.

But of course I haven't understood what was happening, even after everything I've said, everything I've fantasised about. I believed I could see right into her, and she almost believed it too. But now, when she returns home and has become another, or has finally become herself, I don't see it. Her cheeks have been scratched by another man's stubble, but I don't see it. Her hands have done everything I could imagine, everywhere on his body, but I neither smell it nor feel it. She thinks she must tell me, she can't keep it to herself. And then she hears me say it again:

– I want you to do it with him. I know it's going to happen some day. And I want you to come home and tell me about it afterwards.

I am saying it, once more, and it seems unreal to her, disturbing, almost distasteful. She had never thought it could happen, that she could listen to me talk and see me naked and feel such repulsion. I've pulled the duvet aside for her to look at me. I want her to say what she wants to do with him. And she can't tell me what has happened, not now, not while I lie there in the belief that everything that means something to her still involves me, that it is linked to me, to my life. She can't tell me about him, about what they have done. And she suddenly realises that she will never again tell me the most intimate things, this is *her* hereafter, she must take care of it, it can never be mine.

But I am lying beside her, naked now from the waist down. I move onto my side and touch myself. She sees me hold my penis, just like any other man holding himself. She looks at me, she cannot look away. I ask her to tell me more, about what she wants to do with him. And she can't. She can't bring herself to say anything, instead she lies next to me in the bed and listens as I do the talking. It's a kind of story, a fantasy that resembles all my previous fantasies. He arrives at our house, suddenly he's standing there, he has come to visit her. And she hears me say how she leads him into the bedroom, how I am left to stand outside the door listening to her, listening to the sounds she makes while she is naked with another. I seem particularly preoccupied over certain details, that I hear the door being locked, that I hear her shout when she lies under

168

him. And that they start whispering to each other, afterwards, that I can't make out the words, I can only hear the tenderness in their voices.

She has heard all this countless times. Now she listens to me once more, and she watches me masturbate, while I talk about how I'll be made superfluous, how I'll melt into nothing, just watching and listening to what she does with other men. How I shall cease to exist. I am holding my penis, the thought occurs to her that she is seeing this for the last time, it goes white then red then white then red again, I pull the foreskin back and forth, slowly at first and then faster, rhythmically, in a movement somehow disconnected from any other in the world. Soon I'm just a man she has known, one that she lived intimately with, once in an earlier life. She looks at my hand as it moves, fast, fast, up and down, in that unique way that resembles nothing else. Well, yes, it resembles a body itching, a dog scratching behind its ear, its tail slapping rhythmically against the floor. And that's it precisely, she thinks. I'm having a scratch, it'll soon be over, I'm trying to rid myself of a dreadful itch. I'm simply trying to make life a little easier for myself.

With the other hand I pull my T-shirt up over my belly. I want to make myself even more naked for her, or for myself. Besides, I know I'm about to come and I don't want to spoil my clothes. I'm wearing a reasonably new T-shirt, with a print on the front, a glittering blue orange. It doesn't really suit me, my face is too pale for the colour, but I bought it myself, she doesn't buy clothes for me any more. She puts her arm around my shoulder, perhaps to give me some sort of support, a last loving gesture. Perhaps so I'll know that I'm not as alone as I haven't yet realised I actually am, she doesn't quite know herself, she hears me shout with relief. She sees me quiver, and a concentrated spurt of bodily fluid lands white and sticky over my hand, a foul discharge with no purpose flows down the bony back of my hand. An orgasm is like a spontaneous chemical reaction. From a distance it appears small and insignificant, but for the person experiencing the pleasure, it can spread and fill their entire being in a matter of seconds. She watches as my face collapses. My mouth opens, my eyes close, my hand falls powerless onto the sheet. I lie as though I'm dead for a moment, then I come to and tug at the duvet. She helps me to pull it up over my body, and covers me. Watches as I curl up into a ball beneath it. I bring my hands to my face and howl – a desperate, hollow sobbing noise. I am not the man she once knew, I don't even sound like a human being. She lies behind me, her hand still resting on my shoulder. She reminds herself that this will pass, all of it. These are just feelings. Strong feelings, to be sure, violent and bewildering for us both, feelings of total annihilation, so powerful a whole world could go under because of them. And yet sooner or later they will recede, cease to be valid and slowly lose their grip.

HOGARTH
LONDON · NEW YORK

In 1917 Virginia and Leonard Woolf started The Hogarth Press from their Richmond home, Hogarth House, armed only with a hand-press and a determination to publish the newest, most inspiring writing. They went on to publish some of the twentieth century's most significant writers, joining forces with Chatto & Windus in 1946.

Inspired by their example, Hogarth is a new home for a new generation of literary talent; an adventurous fiction imprint with an accent on the pleasures of storytelling and a keen awareness of the world. Hogarth is a partnership between Chatto & Windus in the UK and Crown in the US, and our novels are published from London and New York.